Friend in the Bullseye

A Joth Proctor Fixer Mystery

Books by James V. Irving

The Joth Proctor Fixer *series*
Friends Like These
Friend of a Friend
Friend of the Court
Friend of the Devil
Friend in the Bullseye

Coming Soon!
No Friend of Thine

For more information
visit: www.SpeakingVolumes.us

Friend in the Bullseye

A Joth Proctor Fixer Mystery

James V. Irving

SPEAKING VOLUMES, LLC
NAPLES, FLORIDA
2024

Friend in the Bullseye

Copyright © 2024 by James V. Irving

All rights reserved. No part of this book may be reproduced or transmitted in any form or by any means without written permission.

This is a work of fiction. All incidents and characters are products of the author's imagination. Any resemblance to persons living or dead is coincidental and not intended by the author.

ISBN 979-8-89022-175-9

For Gordon R. Butler and M. Morgan Cherry
two masters of the detective's art

Acknowledgments

Thanks again to my agent Nancy Rosenfeld; to Kurt and Erica Mueller at Speaking Volumes; and to my editor, David Tabatsky.

Thanks to my publicists, Emma Glasgow and Sarah Durrer for their technical skill and energy in the marketing of the Joth Proctor series.

Former Commonwealth Attorney Theo Stamos generously provided several insights on subtleties of the criminal law process that were beyond my personal experience. Thank you, Theo.

Once again, particular thanks to my wife, Cindy.

Chapter One

The Headhunter

Wooded tracts still exist in Arlington County, Virginia, but their number and acreage diminishes year by year, as developers snatch up open spaces to feed the ravenous maw of progress.

Tommy Kuhl, who called himself Arlington's Great White Hunter, lived in a relic of an earlier age: a sprawling, Tudor-style home set well back from the road in a small forest of hardwoods. It had been a remote hunting lodge when Arlington was part of the Confederacy. Now, it was home to one of its most eccentric, narrow-minded, and reviled residents.

Despite his personal unpopularity, Kuhl's annual Halloween party was still the trendy autumn event among Arlington's fashionable crowd, and this was particularly true in an election year. The man knew how to throw a party.

Not being among the in crowd, I first heard about it from Heather's terse voicemail, announcing that she needed an escort. I ignored her request, partly because she was married, and because of her cavalier certainty that I'd have nothing better to do. But she was up for re-election, and she persisted. On her third call, she raised an argument I could not resist.

"He's a well-known bigot," I said. "I wouldn't think you'd want to be associated with him."

"He votes, Joth. And he influences other people who vote."

"So, that's what this is all about? Pressing the flesh?"

"I guarantee Randy Hamburger's going to be there."

Heather was the county's Commonwealth's Attorney. Hamburger was white collar criminal defense lawyer who was running a law-and-order, family values campaign against her.

"I'm not going down without a fight. Everyone there will be a potential vote. I want those people to have a chance to see him next to me, the little weasel."

I took a moment to frame my next question.

"I thought you'd be going with Peter," I said, referring to her husband.

"We're not getting along right now."

I knew more about Heather's marital problems than she suspected, but her secret was safe with me.

"I'm sorry."

"Don't be sorry. Just show up."

And so, I did.

Friend in the Bullseye

***

The sole condition I imposed on my acceptance was that Heather had to drive, because I planned to do some heavy drinking.

It was the last Saturday before Halloween, a dry and windless autumn evening, and just before seven o'clock I heard her honk her horn from the street. We may have been old friends, but Heather wanted to avoid the gossip that could result if she was seen entering my house alone after dark. As I opened the passenger door, I had to stifle a laugh.

"Batgirl?"

She took in my outfit with a glance.

"You look pretty ridiculous yourself."

She engaged the gears before I had my seatbelt buckled and we powered off in a roar.

I had come up with a grim reaper get-up: a hooded black robe, a Guy Fawkes mask, and a plastic scythe on a wooden handle. The scythe just fit between us, angled backward between the bucket seats.

"I hope that's not a comment on my campaign," she said.

She didn't laugh, or even flash a smile, and although she was inscrutable behind the black mask, I sensed anxiety. There were no polls for county-wide elections, but the conventional wisdom suggested she had an uphill climb. Even *The Washington Post's* positive endorsement had been tepid about her chances.

Heather drove a jet-black, five-speed Mustang GT. I used to joke that she wanted the CA job because it would allow her to fix her own speeding tickets. By the way she drove to Kuhl's party, it was only by the grace of good fortune that she didn't have to flex her muscles with the local constabulary.

As she drove, I pulled my hood back and pushed the plastic mask up into my unruly, fast-graying hair.

"I'm sorry about you and Peter."

"Don't get any ideas. It'll work out. Tonight is purely politics."

"Got it."

I was happy to hear her say this for a number of reasons. For one, my life was complicated enough without the possibility of a renewed romantic entanglement with the woman who had become my most trusted friend.

With Heather's attention focused on the road, I took a good look at her costume. She could have pulled off Batgirl with panache ten years earlier, but she was 37 now, a year younger than me to the day, and the years were starting to show. My miles had been harder than hers.

"I wonder what Hamburger will be wearing."

She grinned maliciously.

"I think he'd look great as a Big Mac."

I chuckled, then a silence lingered until she broke it.

"What odds has your buddy Flambeau put on the election?"

Jimmie Flambeau, a gambler and reputed bookie, among other things, had established himself on the edge of the law in Arlington County. He used an artful combination of threats, favors, and money to keep his pockets lined and himself out of trouble. Heather had never found enough evidence to nail him, but she knew he set the money line on anything Arlingtonians were willing to wager a dollar on.

"He's not my friend,"

"He's your client."

"I've got a lot of unpleasant clients."

"Not like him. So, what's the answer?"

"I know he's supporting you."

"That's not what I want to hear."

"He knows enough to keep his preference quiet, but he's spending some money for you."

In the reflected glow of the dashboard, I thought I saw a malicious smile curl her lips. A spirited election fight in his home county would be just the kind of action Jimmie lived for, so I assumed he was taking bets. Heather wanted to know how he handicapped it because she knew he was seldom wrong, and I idly wondered how I could get that information out of him.

She raced through a tight curve and the acceleration forced my head against the headrest.

"I don't get that," she said. "Hamburger would be just the kind of prosecutor Flambeau wants. Law and order will take a back seat to the interests of big business if he's the county's chief prosecutor."

"That's not what Hamburger says."

"Another lying pol!"

I shrugged.

"Devil you know, devil you don't know."

That satisfied her, but it wasn't true. Flambeau believed he had a compromising video of Heather's husband and another woman. He didn't—I'd taken care of that—but as long as he believed it, he'd do what he could to keep Heather in office. If Jimmie had a political bias toward Heather, it was a good thing, regardless of the reason.

She drove on in silence. I sensed something else coming and I waited patiently for it.

"Look, I'm going to lose. I realize that. What do you think about forming a law firm when this is over, you and me?"

I took a gulp of air.

"A law firm?"

"Yeah, a law firm. Burke and Proctor. We'll do nothing but criminal law."

"Proctor and Burke. I've got one more year in the bar than you."

She smiled. I had taken the bait, and realizing this, I backed away.

"Let's wait until the votes are counted, huh?"

She'd planted the seed, and that was enough for one night.

***

The right side of Kuhl's winding country road was lined with expensive, late model cars parked two tires off the roadway with the haphazard unconcern of the very wealthy. Heather slid into a spot, and we stepped out into the autumn air thick with the scents of hickory and oak emanating from the chimneys and firepits of the privileged.

I pulled down my mask, grabbed my scythe and took a good look as Heather swung her legs out of the car and stepped onto the road.

The Batgirl get-up would have been a showstopper during her first election. She was still very pretty, but the years were adding up. She'd grown a little heavy in the hips and thighs, but the slight bulge I'd noticed in her waistline disappeared when she stood up. She pulled the mask over her eyes and the spangles in the strawberry hair that flowed to her shoulders caught the streetlights. She was still capable of turning some heads, mine among them.

The moon, a few days short of full, scudded through the high, cumulous clouds. Across the street, a pair of ornate, wrought iron posts topped by flickering gas lamps marked a gap in the wall of trees. A brick walkway beckoned.

The path that wound through the trees was laid out in a herringbone pattern and I stepped on to it with a heightened sense of curiosity. A soundtrack of classic Halloween hits came piping through the trees and every few yards, a photoelectric sensor set off a ghoulish howl or fiendish laughter. Faux bats dangled from translucent nylon fishing line. Stuffed ravens with blinking yellow eyes roosted in the low branches.

"This might actually be fun," I said.

"It's all business for me. Tonight's the night Hamburger's dreams come crashing down."

"You'd better be careful, or you'll find yourself in a debate with him."

"I've always said I'll debate him anywhere, any place."

"Be careful what you wish for. I hear he's quick on his feet."

"He's a big firm blow hard with pockets deep enough to self-fund. He's used to making wifty promises nobody makes him back up."

Behind the mask, Heather's face had taken on the grim, combative expression I still loved.

"Like I said, this might be fun. Let's focus on that."

Chapter Two

A Kuhl Party

Tommy Kuhl had a reputation for sparing no expense at his annual bash. Mechanical owls hooted and wolves howled as we walked into a fog of dry ice. Farther along, I noticed a heavy, dark object hanging from a tree branch. As we got closer, I realized it was a mannequin dressed in puritan garb, suspended from a noose. I pulled it down and threw it angrily onto the grass. Heather put her hand on my arm.

"Take it easy, Joth. He didn't mean anything by it."

As Heather knew, a Proctor ancestor had been hung for witchcraft in Salem in 1692. More than three centuries had passed since then, but I wasn't going to give Kuhl a pass because of his ignorance. I immediately began plotting how I could give him a piece of my mind without harming Heather's purpose in being here.

"Let me take care of it," she said.

"I thought you were going to take care of Hamburger."

"Bring 'em on. One at a time."

As we continued, glimpses of Kuhl's home appeared between the trees. I recognized it as a Tudor-style chalet that reminded me of a print of a Bavarian hunting lodge. Someone darted by dressed as a mummy. As I turned to comment to Heather, a flash of white flitting between the trees caught my attention. A few paces on, this apparition stepped out into the path. Blonde, lithe and slender, she was dressed in a diaphanous gown over white tights. The gown was replete with shimmering sequins and her face was whitened by pancake make-up. There was a sparkle of glitter in her hair. Two large white wings completed the costume.

"By the twitching of my thumbs…" she said.

Her voice was low, and she looked at Heather.

This frivolous touch lightened my mood and the dark atmosphere of Kuhl's private forest.

"Well, well, who are you?"

"I am Puck."

"Yes, I suppose you are."

She had elegant hands with long fingers, and she pointed one at Heather.

"Beware."

Heather scowled.

"Don't worry. I'm always wary.'"

"Beware of the lamb who comes with the wolf."

With that Parthian shot, she rose on her toes, spun 180 degrees, and with a careless toss of a handful of glitter, disappeared into the trees.

I laughed, the image of hanging witches now exorcized from my mind.

"I told you this would be fun," I said.

"She told me to beware."

"You don't need to beware. You're with the grim reaper."

"Come on. We're late."

The brick path bent sharply before rounding a corner of the stucco and timber home. Beyond this turn, the scene that opened before us was as colorful and active as a Hollywood set.

Kuhl's backyard, ringed in like an amphitheater by trees in their autumn colors, featured a triple terraced flagstone patio, with each semi-circular level enclosed by a low granite wall. Each tier was connected to the one below by a set of broad, granite steps and a series of koi ponds linked by waterfalls. Tiki torches, Japanese lanterns, and strings of yellow lights created a sense of intimacy in the surrounding darkness. The French doors that joined the patio to the house were open, so the party flowed freely between the house and the outside space. It took a lot to impress Heather, but she looked at me and smiled.

"Wow," she said.

One look confirmed what I'd always heard about Kuhl's annual bash, that Arlington's social A-listers took it seriously: Zorro, in his black mask, gaucho hat and cape, leaped from a wall, grinning and brandishing what looked like a real rapier; the Lone Ranger and Tonto, a brooding pair, strode through with the air of armed guards, which they may have been; Dorothy Gale, in gingham jumper, pigtails and ruby slippers, sat with the Cowardly Lion, the Tin Man and the Scarecrow on a pair of wrought iron benches, sharing a joint and giggling uncontrollably; John, Paul, George and Ringo, dressed for their Abbey Road cover shoot, cruised among the crowd; Edgar Allen Poe in a frock coat with a white silk cravat wrapped about his neck, his face eerily pale, staggered about the lower patio, swigging something from a leather flagon.

In addition to the live guests, life-like mannequins in gruesome postures filled several of the benches and green Adirondack chairs. These included Julius Caesar, wearing laurel leaves and a white toga with scarlet trim, a bloody dagger protruding from his neck. Nearby, the crowned and grizzly-bearded Macbeth sat with his head in his lap. From another chair, an apparently inanimate zombie suddenly came to life, stood up and began to dance.

A commotion developed in the middle patio when someone noticed a mannequin in black and white stripped prison garb, a ball and chain around his ankle, lying at the bottom of one of the koi ponds. Where the yard met the woods, George Custer slumped against the trunk of a tree, his cavalry hat pulled low over his blonde-bearded face and a bloody arrow in his chest.

Most of the crowd had congregated on the top level of the patio, where a pair of young men in white dinner jackets were mixing cocktails in silver shakers behind the bars at each end. Even Heather seemed affected by the mood of reckless exuberance.

"Let's get a drink," she said.

I followed her over to the least crowded bar.

"What are you drinking?"

"Same as you."

The bartender was blonde, young, and handsome and he suggested the signature cocktail, which turned out to be something called a Brain Hemorrhage. Heather ordered two.

I was already reconsidering my earlier promise to drink heavily. In college, I welcomed costume parties. They were exciting because you were often unsure who you were talking to behind the mask. That was an enticing prospect for a 20-year-old, but I'd been practicing law so long that the idea of letting my guard down among an anonymous crowd made me nervous.

Nobody had to tell Heather to maintain decorum. The bartender handed her a pair of faux coconut cups. She gave one to me, looked into hers, took a sip, and put it down on top of the granite wall. She was about to speak when a short man in a khaki shirt and shorts and a pith helmet joined us.

"Welcome to the party, Ms. Burke. Always glad to have the law on my side."

She turned toward me, a smile showing beneath the mask.

"Joth, do you know Tommy Kuhl?"

Kuhl puffed out his chest and extended his hand. He wore his sandy blonde hair at a length that would have been fashionable in his teens. He had a pale completion, blues eyes, and even features, but a weak chin gave his face an indecisive cast.

I pushed the mask back from my face.

"I don't appreciate you hanging witches from your trees."

"It's a bit of a sore subject in his family," said Heather.

Kuhl looked at her but ignored her comment. Instead, he blinked and stepped back and Heather took me by the arm. Kuhl eyed me closely.

"It's all in good fun."

"Not to me."

Kuhl tapped a finger against the tip of his nose. He wasn't about to apologize, particularly to some stranger who wasn't even invited to his party. When he was about to speak, probably to invite me to leave, Heather tugged at my elbow.

"Not tonight, my old friend."

I was about to shake her off when Puck appeared at my side.

"Ask to see his heads," she said. "He likes to show off his heads."

Bewildered, I looked at Kuhl, who was smiling indulgently at the girl in white.

"She's right. I do enjoy showing off my heads."

"As in shrunken heads?" said Heather.

He chuckled and his shoulders relaxed. Puck was right. This was a subject he enjoyed. As she ghosted off to haunt someone else, Kuhl began again.

"I am, as you may have heard, a hunter of some distinction."

He looked at his fingernails.

"I've mounted a lot of my kills in the library."

I knew that I had over-reacted, as I tended to do, and Kuhl was trying to patch up a bad start. Nonetheless, the idea of any man, even a hunter of self-described renown, showing off the heads of dead animals left me cold.

"Another time. Maybe."

With a curt nod, I pulled my mask over my face, turned abruptly, and walked away, leaving Heather to make apologies before hurrying after me.

"What the hell's wrong with you?"

I heard her over my shoulder, but I kept walking. Others noticed and a few heads turned. I was no more willing to apologize than Kuhl was, but I didn't want to embarrass Heather, particularly in this most public of settings. I moved quickly down the granite steps toward the lowest and least crowded of the three patios. I knew I was in for a burst of temper when Heather caught up. I wanted to give her a measure of privacy when she unloaded on me.

I stopped at the lowest of the granite walls, where a thin margin of grass separated the patios from the tree line and turned to confront her.

"Nothing's wrong with me. I just don't like that guy."

"You're willing to drink his liquor."

"I came here as a favor to you."

"Okay, he's a poseur with the resources to indulge his insecurities. Hemingway had the same hobby."

"That was decades ago. There are a lot of things people did then that don't fly now."

"Does that make him any different from you?"

She smiled. She was goading me. It was one of the things Heather was good at.

"Alright. I overreacted. But you know that witch thing…"

She put a hand on my arm.

"I know. It's a third rail for you. Just pass it off to a weird guy with macabre taste. But it's Halloween. People get away with a lot of things on Halloween. Just look around. Everybody's having a great time. They can't get enough of this stuff."

As we turned together to take in the brightly lit scene, a skeleton reclining on a chaise suddenly stood up, shocking the fairy princess seated on the wall beside him. He danced away toward the bar. Nearby, a devil in a red body suit, complete with forked tail, forehead horns and a full-face, fiendish mask, was dancing provocatively with Little Red Riding Hood in a scarlet hood and cape and a domino mask.

Amused, I turned to say something to Heather, but her body had turned rigid. She cocked her head and lifted her nose like a blood hound on a scent. I cast a glance at Dorothy's little circle and was about to comment on the status of marijuana use in the commonwealth when

Heather suddenly took three long strides toward the form of Colonel Custer, propped against the tree at the edge of the circle of light.

He was dressed in tan riding pants, Wellington boots, and a fringed buckskin coat. A yellow bandana was tied loosely around his neck. His buff-colored cavalry hat was pulled down to his nose, revealing a neat, tawny beard. Yellow curls peeked out from under the hat. The arrow in his chest was an obvious toy and the blood that soaked his chest looked like ketchup.

As Heather quickly pushed the hat back from his face, I heard her suck in her breath. She reached down, took Custer's wrist and felt for his pulse. She straightened and took a long step back. As she did, I saw that the body was Randy Hamburger, and he was just as dead as George Armstrong Custer.

Chapter Three

The Path Forward

Word spread quickly among the party goers. The costumed crowd disbursed as if someone had shouted "fire" in a crowded theater. Heather was a rock among the terrified, and as she took charge, I stayed with her.

The short arrow affixed to Randy Hamburger's tattersall shirt had a suction cup on the other end, which looked like part of a children's play set. He was dead, alright, but he hadn't been killed with an arrow. By the way she smelled his lips, I could see that Heather was considering the possibility of poison. The police were on the scene within minutes and quickly reached the same preliminary conclusion. I gave a statement to one of the first officers to arrive. As soon as I completed it, Heather asked me if I could find a ride home.

I glanced at Hamburger and the med techs and detectives still gathered around him.

"Maybe I should stay."

Heather's eyes narrowed.

"I can get an officer to drive you home if you can't find a ride."

I took the hint, but instead of leaving, I walked up the two sets of granite stairs and through the open French doors into the house. Inside, the wide, high ceilinged central hallway was brighter than day. In a doorway to the left, a pair of cops were quietly comparing notes. They both looked up and one of them recognized me.

"Joth Proctor. What are you doing here?"

It was Christine Kelleher, an attractive, robust officer who had been on Jimmie Flambeau's payroll, and maybe still was.

"Doing my job, just like you."

She was aware that I knew of her relationship to Jimmie's operation and that made her circumspect. She was unconvinced, but she tilted her head, waiting for more explanation.

"I'm here to see Tommy Kuhl. Do you know where I can find him?"

"Client of yours?"

I gave her a conspiratorial wink.

"Well, we'll see. More like a friend right now."

She shrugged. Christine had more important things to do than to judge the motives of a lawyer at a crime scene.

"He's in the library."

She jerked a thumb over her shoulder, and I headed that way.

Halfway down the hallway, a pair of floor-to-ceiling doors of polished oak with heavy gold handles had been thrown open. I stuck my head in. The room was paneled in ornately carved fruitwood that glowed with the reflected blaze from a broad, fieldstone fireplace. Along one long wall, floor to ceiling bookshelves were lined with books that had the look of unread sets picked up at estate sales.

Tommy was seated in a red leather armchair at the side of the fireplace. He was leaning forward, elbows on his knees, his head in his hands. He looked up when he heard me approach. The pith helmet was gone, and I saw that his sandy hair, long and luxuriant over his ears and neck, was rapidly receding on the top.

"Hello, Proctor."

The awkward moment from earlier in the evening was forgotten.

"Hi Tommy. Are you alright?"

"Pretty shaken, if you want to know the truth."

I glanced up at the enormous, mounted head of a roaring lion above the mantlepiece, and at the lesser trophy heads that decorated the other walls. This was a man who'd seen death before, but not like this, not human death on his own property.

"Is he really dead?"

Tommy's leather chair had a twin on the other side of the fireplace. I took it.

"Yeah, he's dead."

"I hope nobody thinks that was one of my arrows."

I processed his comment. He didn't seem to realize the arrow was a toy.

"You're a bow hunter?"

"Yes."

I looked again at the array of heads, including the male lion. It took a brave man to kill a lion with a bow and arrow. Or a man with a lot of money and a brave guide.

"Did you give the cops a statement?"

"Yeah."

"Did they read you your rights?"

"Yes."

I was mildly surprised. It would have been easy to tell Tommy that the arrow was a prop and not the cause of death. Instead, the cops were letting him twist in the wind. It looked like somebody liked Kuhl even less than I did, and I wondered if that someone was Officer Kelleher.

As Tommy sat back in his chair, the firelight caught the ring on the little finger of his right hand: a yellow diamond in a platinum setting. He didn't have the sort if hands you'd want to call attention to, aged-splotched and veined, with crooked fingers that bespoke a life of broken bones. But he wasn't the sort of person to acknowledge the fraying of the aging process.

"Should I be worried?"

I took a breath to slow us both down.

"How well did you know Hamburger?"

He paused.

"I hardly knew him at all."

I let that sink in.

"You invited him to your party."

"Sure. I invite all the players."

"Did you have a chance to talk to him?"

"I didn't even know he was here."

"So, someone's trying to set you up?"

He looked up, startled at the suggestion.

"Me?"

"Tommy, you've got a dead man lying in your yard. How do you figure it?"

He blew out his breath and let his head wag, as if the effort was too much for him.

"I don't know. Somebody put him there."

"Somebody who's got it in for you, Tommy. Any idea who that could be?"

"No. These mannequins, even the witch you didn't like; people bring them. They put them up here and there or in the bottom of one of the ponds, so they surprise everyone. It's been part of the fun for years."

"Any idea how long he'd been there?"

"Hamburger? I never noticed him at all."

There was a whiff of untruth in his voice and body language, but he was shaken, probably too shaken to lie.

I had another question, but before I could pose it, a shadow fell from the doorway across the rug. It was Heather.

"I thought I told you to go home."

I leaned back in the chair and folded one leg over the other.

"You did. But then I ran into Tommy."

"Beat it, Proctor. This is a police scene."

Her tone and language signaled an end to the easy familiarity of the first part of evening. Work trumped everything with her. It always had.

I considered telling Heather I represented Kuhl. I was confident he'd embrace the prospect of a shield between himself and the investigating authorities, but I didn't want to lock myself into that relationship. There were too many ways this case could play out.

I got up and left with nods to both of them. Heather sat down across from Kuhl in the chair I had vacated. I headed toward the French doors and the backyard, knowing she was about to wring Tommy dry.

All the guests had gone except a handful still conversing with the police. The patio showed signs of hurried flight, like an athletic field after the last game of a lost season. Coconut shaped cups, upright and overturned, and pieces of costumes littered the flagstone. The tiki torches had been doused, but the Japanese lanterns and strings of lights still burned brightly, and light poured out through the open French doors.

The med techs and detectives pored over the patio and yard with their usual painstaking care. The area around the tree where Hamburger had been found was marked off with yellow police tape, but Hamburger's body was long gone. I walked up to the tape and took a careful look around with the aid of the flashlight in my phone, but except for trampled grass, there was nothing for me to pick up. That was okay. What I wanted to investigate was the area behind the tree.

Tommy had suggested that guests were encouraged to participate by bringing and displaying their own ghosts and ghouls and similar spooky favors. I reasoned that most of these would have been delivered by the first wave of guests who found a place for their contribution and used the opportunity to get a head start on their drinking.

Whoever had brought the dead or dying body of Randy Hamburger wouldn't have risked mingling with the early guests using the brick-lined path from the street. That would explain why Hamburger had been placed at the very back of the yard. Someone had come through the woods, quickly propped him against the tree, and just as quickly departed or joined the party.

What I wanted to know was where that person had come from. After a quick look to see if anyone was watching, I stepped behind the tree and into the woods.

Sure enough, illuminated by my flashlight and the occasional light of the moon as it peeked through the trees, I was able to discern a narrow, winding path that was probably the work of neighborhood kids. I followed it. About 50 yards back, a small trunk path branched off to a circular clearing. There was a labyrinth in the center of the clearing; a maze of dirt pathways lined with flat stones, all of which led to dead ends but for a single path leading to an unlit firepit in the center.

Wiccans?

I got back on the main path and followed it through the woods until it popped out in the back of a residential cul-de-sac. It was paved, but without sidewalks or gutters, and was home to a quartet of contemporary, three-story houses on large lots. I looked at my watch. It was a little late to be knocking on doors, especially dressed as the Grim Reaper.

Before I turned to go, I took a last look around. There was something about the neighborhood that seemed familiar. For a moment, I wondered if I'd been here before, but I shook that off. It was identical to dozens of "exclusive" neighborhoods that had popped up in 21st century Arlington, all from the same set of cookie cutter designs.

I called an Uber, then walked back through the woods, and down the brick path out to Tommy Kuhl's now empty road, where I caught a ride home.

Chapter Four

The Arrow Points to Heather

The press coverage of Hamburger's death was immediate and heavy. Although I'd given a statement at Kuhl's, another police investigator showed up at my office Monday morning. I told him the same thing I'd told the detective on the scene, which wasn't much. As I had on Saturday night, I stopped my statement when I got to Heather's discovery of Hamburger's body. I decided to keep that part of what I knew to myself and managed to do so without lying.

About an hour later, Heather called and asked me to lunch, as I knew she would. She'd made a habit of bouncing thoughts and ideas off me, particularly in high profile cases. Because of my presence at the scene, there were several overlays to this request.

I suggested Ireland's Four Courts, a place close to the courthouse and both our offices, but Heather demurred.

"I was thinking of that Chinese place in Vienna we used to go to."

Vienna was 20 minutes away and outside her jurisdiction, and I immediately understood that this was the point. The last thing she wanted was to meet at a public place where someone might see her talking to me. But she lived in Arlington, and her kids went to school there. She'd have no peace in her hometown until Hamburger's murder was solved.

Wu's Garden was a cozy place with a traditional Chinese motif and booths around the walls, enclosing a large, square room of four-top tables. It was a spot we used to go to for cashew chicken back when we were dating. Tucked into a strip shopping center on busy Maple Avenue, it was small and quiet, and that's what Heather wanted both then and now.

She was waiting for me at a booth in the back, and her cup of green tea was almost empty. The appetizing scents of garlic, soy, and ginger wafted in the air, and suddenly I was back in an earlier era.

I sat down and ordered coffee.

"Did you get any sleep this weekend?"

She made a wry face. Heather was a stunning woman even on a bad day, but I saw the signs of the building pressure.

"Not much. How 'bout you?"

"Slept like a baby."

She sneered. Heather's nerves were on edge, and it didn't take her long to come to the point. After the waiter took our order and moved away, she leaned toward me.

"Whoever killed Hamburger did it before the party started. They carried him in and leaned him against the tree."

She wanted my reaction. She watched me to assess if she was telling me something I already knew or assumed.

"That's pretty bold. While the caterers were setting up?"

"Maybe. People were busy, active. Other mannequin cadavers were being placed, so one more wouldn't have garnered any special attention."

"How'd you happen to notice him?"

"I've smelled enough corpses to recognize the scent."

"How long had he been dead?"

"The lab's checking that now."

I was sure the lab had already done that, and that she knew the answer. It was good to know the limits of her confidence.

"What kind of poison?"

"What difference does it make?"

That was an odd statement coming from Heather, who would normally be immersing herself in every fact and factor, no matter how obscure.

My pause registered and she caught her breath.

"Yeah, I'm anxious. It's not every day your opponent gets killed just before the election."

That was the coincidence that had occupied my mind all weekend, and I was sure it had been hers as well.

"What happens now? Will there be a substitute candidate?"

"Too late. The ballots have already been printed and early voting has begun."

Two days before, defeat seemed certain. Now, everything had changed.

"So, you're a shoo-in?"

"I prefer not to think of it that way. Or talk of it that way. It just means I need to be sure to nail whoever did it."

So, this was the end of Proctor and Burke. I felt a twinge of disappointment, and that surprised me.

"Suspects?"

"None yet. I'm making a list of people with a motive. It's a pretty long list."

I could imagine. Hamburger was not a popular man. His scorched earth tactics, combined with his reputation for pressing his defendants to plead guilty in cases he wasn't sure of winning, had left him with plenty of dissatisfied clients.

Of course, Heather, being the person with the most to gain, would be on top of most people's suspect lists. I left that point unmade, but I was sure that fact was never far from the front of her mind.

"Most of the logical suspects are in jail."

She smiled and nodded.

"But not all of them."

"The ones who aren't might be a good place to start," I said.

"I've already told Crandall to look into it."

Sue Crandall, Heather's chief deputy, was also the person having an affair with Heather's husband.

I suspected that Heather had already assumed that someone had lugged Hamburger those 75 yards through the woods just as bartenders, caterers and early arrivals were gearing up. If so, she also had probably discovered the path to the neighborhood. Hamburger wasn't a big guy, but whoever pulled that off had both nerve and a good bit of physical strength.

"Why deposit the body at Kuhl's party?"

"Maybe someone doesn't like Tommy," she said.

"From what I hear, that's another pretty long list."

"Or maybe somebody wanted to make a big splash."

"Heather, he was the leading candidate for chief prosecutor in this county. He could have drowned in his bathtub, and it would have made a big splash."

When lunch came, the conversation slowed. Each of us hoped to learn what the other knew or thought without giving too much away. Since I didn't represent her, Heather couldn't know who might one day put me under oath and demand details of our conversations. That was an ugly prospect for both of us. It was the reason I didn't ask her if she'd been to the cul-de-sac.

"I assume you're going to recuse yourself from the investigation?"

"No. I'm the only person in the office capable of handling this case."

"Come on, Heather, you've got a stable of qualified assistants. You've trained them yourself."

"It takes more than trial skills to handle a case like this."

She was right about that. Hamburger's murder would occupy a big stage under the bright lights of public scrutiny. And her office's relationship to the victim made it critical that they nail the killer. Any failure would be pinned on Heather whether she handled the case or not.

"So, you'll oversee it from the background?"

A furrow of wrinkles appeared between her eyebrows. She was annoyed, and after stifling it for a moment, her anger flared.

"No! I've been the CA for almost a decade. You think anybody really thinks I murdered that loser? It's not like I'd have no life if I lost!"

I wondered briefly if she'd feel the same way if she was sharing rent with me on a suite in DP Tran's cinderblock cubbyhole.

Then I resorted to the ethics argument of last resort.

"It's not a conflict, but there may be an appearance of conflict…"

"Drop it, Joth. I'm tired of hearing about it."

"So, somebody else is making the same argument?"

She pushed her plate away and glared at me. Now, I knew why she had asked me to lunch. She wanted to assess whether she could withstand the pressure that others would bring and were already bringing to bear on her if she stayed in the case. She didn't say anything, but her expression told me that she knew the answer and it wasn't what she had hoped to hear.

"Look, Joth. My hands are tied. You're the best person in the county to get to the bottom of this. I want you to figure it out. Will you do that for me?"

I thought about telling her that I already had enough non-paying clients, but there were a lot of reasons why I wouldn't turn this one down. It was a juicy, high-profile case and it would generate the kind of press that often determines the level of a defense lawyer's success. Plus, it would keep me close to Heather, both professionally and personally.

"You want to hire me?"

"Are you going deaf?"

It was a good idea. For one thing, if I was her attorney, our strategic discussions would be privileged and shielded from disclosure.

"Alright."

"Have Marie send me a retainer agreement. I'll pay your normal deposit for a case like this. We're going to do this by the book."

"Sure."

She didn't have to tell me that. Heather did everything by the book.

Chapter Five

Stuck with Her

The other call I expected came just after noon the following day. It was Sue Crandall, and when Marie announced the call, I guessed that she and Heather had been arguing all morning. She'd waited until Heather was at lunch before trying to leverage me.

I picked up on my desk line. Sue didn't beat around the bush. She never did.

"She's going to have to recuse herself, you know."

I used her impatience and excitement against her.

"Who's going to have to recuse herself from what?"

"You know what I'm talking about! She can't handle the Hamburger case. She's a witness."

"And an interested party. So what? Who's going to object?"

Crandall was dumbfounded by my audacity. It took her a moment to marshal her thoughts.

"You can't be serious, Joth! She can't investigate the murder of her political rival!"

"I suppose you think it should be you? The deputy who's screwing her husband?"

"Was."

"When did you stop? Sunday morning?"

Her toned softened, but she did not let up. Sue lacked her boss's ability to connect with people, judges, jurors, witnesses, but she was a bulldog. Heather had strengths and qualities that most court watchers took for granted, but the citizens of Arlington County would miss her personal touch when and if she was gone.

"I'm going to handle this, Joth. Talk to her, before she does something stupid."

She'd made her point, and I'd made mine. Crandall was somewhat vulnerable, but she was also right. If Heather didn't recuse herself from the investigation, either the presiding judge or the bar ethics committee would insist on it. More important, people would wonder why she hadn't taken this obvious step without being pushed. Inaction would suggest she had something to hide. She'd see that herself in time, but she didn't have that luxury. She had to be the first to reach this obvious conclusion, not the last.

"I don't need to talk to her. She'll do the right thing."

With that ambiguous comment, I hung up, just as Sue was starting to reply.

I gave Heather time to get back from lunch, then called her cell. That was not my usual practice, and I assumed she'd see the break in protocol as a sign of urgency. She didn't, or she didn't seem to.

"Got time for coffee?"

"Sure. You coming over here?"

"I was thinking of Willard's."

She was silent for a long moment as she absorbed the unspoken message. Willard's, a local coffeehouse, was the place she took reluctant witnesses to soften them up, or to put the screws to difficult lawyers.

Finally, she responded.

"I'm betting you got a call from my deputy."

Her ability to read people and anticipate their moves was one of the reasons she was such a good prosecutor.

"Then I don't need to tell you what she said."

"You think she's right, don't you?"

"Let's have that cup of coffee."

It had been as little over a month since my last visit to Willard's, when I'd been assaulted by a local thug. He might have killed me if it hadn't been for the quick reaction of Raighne Youngblood, the large, quiet, combat vet who seemed to be Willard's only barista. As I walked in, he nodded as if it had never happened and turned to brew me a pumpkin spiced latte. That was alright with me. I could still feel the thug's big hands around my throat.

Willard's was owned by the Virginia attorney general's office, a secret lair of the state's law enforcement establishment that DP Tran had ferreted out. The interior was cool and dim. Raighne was about as talkative as a cigar store Indian, but he had once told me this was to keep the electric bills down. I assumed it was because the things that went down in Willard's were best done in the dark. I waited at the bar for my latte and carried it to a table in the far corner.

Once Heather got past the initial shock of Hamburger's murder, I expected relief to float up through her weariness. While Hamburger's murder fell under her jurisdiction, she was now certain to keep her job with only a dead man's name across from hers on the ballot. Instead, she was angry, and nobody got angry like Heather Burke. The ever-astute Raighne had her tea at the table almost before she sat down.

I began to relate the call from Sue, but Heather cut me off.

"You see? That bitch is already maneuvering to push me aside."

"She's the logical choice to sub in for you, Heather. It seems to me she's trying to resolve it quickly and quietly. Your office is known for no-nonsense efficiency. If there's infighting, it'll get out, and you don't want that."

It was a chilly day, and she'd come without a jacket. She warmed her hands around the ceramic cup. Then, she took a long sip of tea and thoughtfully printed rings of moisture on the napkin.

"I know. I don't mind stepping back. I just don't want Sue handling the investigation."

"Why not? She's your deputy. That's her job."

"I don't trust her."

"How come she's your deputy?"

She didn't look up.

"It's complicated."

For a moment, I wondered if she had found out about Crandall and her husband, but if she was letting Sue blackmail her, it would have meant she was desperate to preserve her marriage. I put that thought out of my mind.

"I should have fired her a year ago."

"Well, you didn't, and now you're stuck with her."

"There's a guy named Bill Duncan out in the valley. Good prosecutor. Maybe I could bring him in."

"I know him. Organized, smart and tough. But bringing him in would raise a lot of questions. Like why Sue got passed over."

"Yeah, I know."

Heather didn't want to hear these questions. She sighed and pushed away from the table.

"I guess I'm stuck with her. The problem is, she really isn't that good."

"That's not it. You don't want to lose control."

She shrugged off my barb.

"That's partly true. I like to run these big investigations myself. They're used to that downstairs."

"You aren't saying the cops have forgotten how to do it?"

"No, but something is … well, you know."

What she was saying was that powerful interests sometimes try to put a thumb on the scale of justice.

"Hamburger had a lot of enemies."

"No kidding. Juggling them might be the hardest part, and seeing subtle shades of grey is not Sue's strength."

"Don't forget, you'll still be the Commonwealth's Attorney. She's only going to run this one case."

"But this case is the problem. That's why I need you, Joth."

"Alright. Consider me your lawyer. You can count on that. But let's keep it quiet. I don't want anyone asking why you need a lawyer."

"Don't be simple minded. I had the most to gain by the murder."

"Yeah, but that's…"

"Crandall's wanted my job for years. That's no secret. If she can find and convict the killer, she'll use that success to run against me in the next election."

So, this was what was making her anxious. I didn't like Crandall any more than Heather, but I could be a bit more objective about her.

"This'll be just another closed case in four years."

"It better be. But if it's not, Sue will make sure I get the blame."

I sighed. But now that I was Heather's attorney, we could speak more frankly.

"Okay. Let me ask you a question. Did you get a chance to explore the woods behind where they found Hamburger?"

"No. Should I have?"

"It might have been tough in those Batgirl boots. But I did. There's a small neighborhood on the other side of those trees. I think somebody may have staged the murder from there."

"Did you check it out?"

"Of course. There are four houses there. I'll get DP to run background checks on all the residents. Maybe knock on some doors."

She nodded, and I sipped my latte as a way of signaling a change in topics.

"Heather, even assuming you're right about Crandall; you don't think there are people in the courthouse who'd work against you?"

She shrugged, and I saw that she'd already thought it through.

"One thing about the courthouse. You can think you know what's going on, but you really have no idea. There are too many people with personal agendas."

"By the way, what do we know about the poison?"

"Strychnine."

I took in some air. Strychnine! That was a fast-working and deadly alkaloid. An oral dose of three milligrams could kill a man Hamburger's size within minutes. Typically, it's mixed with something else to disguise the taste and it's administered orally.

"It's what they used to kill Alexander the Great, you know."

She rolled her eyes.

"Did DP tell you that?"

"In fact, he did."

"I'll bet he told you he was there."

I ignored her.

"Strychnine causes convulsions, paralysis and then asphyxiation. Is that what we have here?"

"That's what pathology says."

"Well, that's a good starting point. Any idea where it came from?"

"Nope. At least I don't."

"I assume Sue's working on that, too."

She threw up her arms.

"I just don't trust her, Joth."

"Just let it go. Your interests are the same. Take my advice and don't worry about it."

"I hate to admit it, Joth, but you are usually right."

At least I was this time. Heather recused herself from the investigation of Randy Hamburger's murder. There was no public announcement. Heather handed off the file to Crandall and people heard about it on a need-to-know basis.

Life would go on as usual at the Arlington Commonwealth's Attorney's office. Then again no; I knew better than that.

Chapter Six

The Temptation of Steady Pay

Many people in the county knew who Jimmie Flambeau was, though few had met him. Jimmie wanted it that way and he preferred to have people like me around to provide a buffer to enforce that separation.

During the summer, when things were running smoothly between Jimmie and me, he'd put me on a $5,000 a month retainer to lock me into fixing any of the little headaches that often bedevil someone in his line of work. For Jimmie, it was a small price to pay to assure that all our discussions were protected by attorney-client privilege.

He was an unscrupulous man and an uncommon crook, but I was willing to sign on to his payroll because he was a ready source of information on a variety of subjects not otherwise available. Plus, I thought $5,000 a month was a lot of money. Dealing with Jimmie was like dancing with the devil: a high octane mix of possible risk and reward.

Friend in the Bullseye

When Jimmie called me late in the afternoon his voice was jovial and boisterous, so I knew he wanted something.

"Cut to the chase, Jimmie. I've got a client coming in ten minutes."

"Are we still on the retainer?"

"Apparently not. You haven't paid me for October."

He swore and slammed the desk. Under the retainer relationship, I performed varied legal tasks for him as requested, with my total monthly fees equal to the amount of the agreed deposit. This meant there was no written trail of formal assignments or the legal guidance I gave him in return. Both of us found this preferrable when the work sometimes pushed up against what the law permitted. Advice of counsel is the last refuge of the scoundrel.

"I'll tell Helen to get you a check for $5,000 today."

I'm not a shrewd negotiator on my own behalf, but it was different with Jimmie. He expected it, and besides, I didn't like him.

"Six thousand a month."

"I think it's five."

"Prices have gone up."

"Five. And it's easy money."

"Last time, it was mostly collecting rent from your deadbeat tenants. That's ugly work."

"Five thousand-five hundred. Are you in or out?"

"Something's eating you, Jimmie. What is it?"

"To tell you the truth, it's that murder last week."

That set off alarm bells.

"What about it?"

"Five thousand-five hundred."

"Six."

"Christ on a shingle!"

I heard him jab the intercom.

"Helen, get me a six-thousand-dollar check for Mr. Proctor."

I wanted to think that Jimmie's willingness to jump the price was a measure of his respect for my competence, but I knew better. It was a measure of his concern.

"Okay, Jimmie, you're back on. Now, let's have it."

"This is confidential, right?"

That kind of question always promised danger. I thought about my answer, but there was only one possible response. Jimmie was a legitimate client, and he was asking for legal advice.

"Yes. What's the issue?"

"I was at Kuhl's party Saturday night."

"I didn't see you there."

"I was the devil."

I remembered the horned character in the bright red costume grinding away with Little Red Riding Hood.

"What else?"

"That's it."

"That's it?"

"I just said that."

Nobody was going to tie Jimmie Flambeau to the murder just because he'd been at the scene, disguised or not.

"I don't think you've got much to worry about."

"If Burke finds out, she's going to try to pin it on me."

"Heather doesn't work that way."

"I just want to know that you're in it for me in case someone starts asking questions that are tough to answer."

Heather wanted the same thing. She and Jimmie viewed me less as a lawyer than as a fixer; someone brought in to put out fires and solve problems before they developed.

For a moment, I considered the conflict that representing both could pose. Jimmie wasn't a suspect, despite his concerns, and Heather probably wouldn't be either, even if some people might prefer it that way.

Seeing that business was slow, Jimmie's monthly check would look nice and tidy in my bank account.

"You got anything more to tell me?"

"Come over. Helen will have the check ready for you."

I pulled on the tweed sport coat that hung behind my door and headed up the street. As I darted across Wilson Boulevard, I wondered what tough questions Jimmie anticipated, and who he expected to be asking them.

***

It was a bright and balmy fall afternoon. The crisp air energized me with a sense that opportunities awaited. Jimmie office suite was on the top floor of a six-story building in the same neighborhood as my humble accommodations. The door was unmarked and located by the sixth-floor restrooms, where no curious or distracted visitor to the large, adjacent law firm would be likely to stumble into it.

I didn't bother to knock. The area immediately outside the entrance was covered by surveillance equipment and I knew that Helen, Jimmie's gorgeous secretary, monitored it religiously. Before I could count to five, I heard the click of the security bolt slipping back. I stepped inside.

Helen smiled, which wasn't her usual practice.

"Looks like you missed me," I said.

She didn't appreciate sarcasm. She returned her attention to her computer screen.

"He's back there. You know the way."

I assumed that was the last smile I'd get from her for a while.

Jimmie was small, trim, intense man with dark eyes and hair. Always well-dressed and groomed, he was wearing a gray turtleneck under a blue blazer and his tiny hands looked recently manicured. He was studying something on a laptop set up on his oversized desk and he motioned me to one of the chrome-framed chairs across from him.

In the corner to the right of the chair stood the heavy duty safe that Jimmie believed contained the video of Heather's husband and Sue Crandall. I knew better, but that wasn't what I was interested in. Earlier in the fall, I'd seen a valuable impressionist painting hanging above the safe that I knew had been stolen from a museum in Boston in 1990. Now, a Currier & Ives calendar hung in that spot, opened to the September scene of hunters and their retrievers gathered around a campfire.

Jimmie turned to me, but his beady eyes were glassy and distracted.

"Something bothering you, Jimmie?"

He made a dismissive gesture and snapped out of it. "No. Of course not."

I didn't want to let it go. It was a rare thing to catch him at a disadvantage. College football was one of his major lines of business.

"Did you mess up the odds on the Alabama game?"

He glared at me.

"I told you, it's nothing."

I wasn't sure I'd ever seen Jimmie angry except when he wanted to be, so I knew I was on to something. He pushed the check across to me with a surly expression and without meeting my eyes. Whatever the problem was, it would soon be mine. I studied the check.

"So, this is about Saturday night? You want to talk about it?"

"He was the law-and-order candidate who was gonna restore family values in the community. I was there dressed as the devil on the night he got killed."

"Who knows about that?"

He swiveled toward the window and its dramatic view of a colorful canopy of trees that made a collage of the Virginia countryside.

"I was taking bets on the election. That's not a secret. Anybody with a brain knows that I'd get hurt if he won. I'm an obvious target for a new prosecutor trying to make his bones."

Hamburger's campaign commitment to criminal justice would be forgotten as soon as the votes were counted. Jimmie may not have understood this. But he also didn't know that he no longer had the compromising video of Crandall and Heather's husband.

"What do you want me to do?"

"Keep me out of it. That's all. Just keep me out of it."

"Okay. There's nothing to worry about right now. I'll stay on top of it."

I waited a moment, but he seemed to have forgotten me. I stood up and he let me leave without another word.

Jimmie had the balls of a brass monkey, so whatever was bothering him was worth knowing. Out in the reception area, I perched on the edge of Helen's desk and nodded in the direction of Jimmie's office.

"I don't want you to worry too much about it. I'll take care of it."

Her lovely green eyes sparkled. Jimmie kept her so thoroughly in the dark that she had no idea what or how much of any subject Jimmie revealed to me.

"I don't know much about it."

"I know."

I winked and she smiled hopefully.

"I think I can cover it. How did it happen?"

She shrugged.

"I don't know. He sounded anxious when he called."

"He didn't call Jimmie directly?"

She vehemently shook her lovely head.

"He's never given him his direct number."

"He will when he learns to trust him."

"*If,* you mean. I know he trusts you. But he doesn't feel that way about McGriff."

I stood up. So, it was Ish McGriff who'd delivered whatever news had distracted Jimmie Flambeau. I wondered if Ish knew something about what happened Saturday night, or how the county authorities were pursuing it.

"Well, we'll see if we can't put some sort of failsafe in place for next time."

"Thanks, Joth."

She'd never used my first name before. Maybe I'd made an ally, but I'd once thought that about Ish, too. Now, I had to figure out what bad news Ish McGriff had delivered.

Chapter Seven

Two Guilty Men

Ish McGriff was a sheriff's deputy. In that capacity, he'd recently shot and killed a man suspected of murder, a man who also once worked for Jimmie Flambeau. Following the shooting, Ish had been out for two weeks on administrative leave. The shooting had been quickly ruled self-defense, but the sheriff had been troubled enough by the circumstances to take Ish off the street. Now he worked in the courthouse, and I suspected that whatever had spooked Jimmie had come from there. There wasn't much else that bothered him.

I knew that I needed to speak to Ish before he talked to Jimmie again, so I went directly to the courthouse. The parking lot across Courthouse Road was busy with the usual crowd of late arriving jurors, defendants, and witnesses jockeying for limited parking spaces, which I negotiated like the midfield of a lacrosse field on a fast clear.

The sheriff's office was on the first floor of the jail, a six-floor tower across the plaza from the courthouse building. I knew the desk sergeant. I smiled, glanced at my watch and told him I had lunch plans with deputy McGriff, which was true as far as it went. The only lie was that McGriff wasn't aware of those plans.

The sergeant consulted a sheet posted on the pinboard at the front of his cubicle.

"He's got security in Hawkins' courtroom this week."

I wonder if Jimmie had arranged that. Courtroom bailiff was a good place to stick an informant. I nodded and looked again at my watch. It was 11:45 a.m. and I was in luck. Hawkins was very particular about the timing of lunch time recess.

"That's what I thought. Thanks, Sergeant."

Hawkins was a district judge with a courtroom on the third floor. I loitered in the lobby, passing the time by chatting with a young lawyer who was waiting for a chance to talk to a prosecutor. He asked if I'd been at Kuhl's party Saturday night, and when I admitted I had, I couldn't get him off the topic until just after noon, when the courtroom door opened, and a sullen procession of defendants and their lawyers filed out in ones and twos. After securing the courtroom and locking up, McGriff was the last to leave.

"Hey, Ish."

McGriff was an unusually handsome man with the size and strength of a defensive end. He had a bright and engaging smile that he knew how to employ to set a disarming tone, but I was getting none of that today. He was too shrewd to believe this was a coincidence.

"What are you doing here?"

"You got time for lunch?"

He gave it a moment's thought while giving me a hard look. Ish's mocha-colored skin gleamed under the bright lights of the courtroom lobby. His dark brown, short sleeved shirt was crisply pressed, and it fit him like a glove. His brawny arms were covered with tattoos.

"You buying?"

"Sure."

"Ragtime?"

"I was thinking the same thing."

I'm just over six feet and a former college lacrosse player, but I felt small in Ish's confident presence. He was familiar with the aura he projected and enjoyed its effect.

Ragtime was just around the corner, and we walked over together without speaking, each waiting for the other to open the conversation. Courthouse personnel enjoyed preference at the tavern, so the hostess quickly found us a booth.

Ish McGriff had killed a man, and so had I. We shared this guilt like original sin, and I knew the implacable sense of disgust and self-loathing that branded a killer for life. As we sat, I searched Ish's face for a flicker of the bitterness that had infected me, but there was no sign of it. I understood the difference: Ish's sin was public, and he had been absolved by the authorities. There could be no similar redemption for me.

I relaxed, took a breath and studied the room. Beneath the clatter of cutlery and cheap china, a chowder of urgent, whispered conversations bubbled up: lawyers with their anxious clients, lawyers with forgetful witnesses, lawyers twisting other lawyer's arms.

I ordered coffee. Ish ordered tea. We both ordered the special: BLT and she-crab soup.

"How are the girls?"

I asked about his daughters in an attempt to create a bond, but the comment only heightened his suspicions.

"Don't waste my time, Joth."

Late in the summer, Jimmie had hired me to collect overdue rent from Ish. I had negotiated a fair arrangement on the rent deficiency, but when the two of them struck an alliance, my efforts went by the wayside. During that representation, I had learned a lot about Ish and his family, and I wanted to remind him of that. My question also was a way of saying no hard feelings, but Ish chose not to take it that way.

"Okay."

Friend in the Bullseye

A pretty, redheaded waitress in a short, dark green dress brought our order. I munched a French fry.

"I'm working for Jimmie again. You probably know that."

"What makes you think I'd know that?"

"Look Ish, I'm just trying to earn my money. You know how I work."

"I got nothing to tell you."

"I know Jimmie's in a pinch."

That suggestion elicited nothing. Ish took a big bite out of his sandwich.

"You want me to ask Kelleher?"

Christine Kelleher, the Arlington cop I'd bumped into at Kuhl's party, was also on Jimmie's payroll, or had been. I wanted Ish to believe I could be a resource to whichever of them wanted to exploit the connection. Jimmie paid for information, and if I could give it to her instead of Ish, that decreased Ish's value to Jimmie. But he surprised me, focusing not on what I had to offer, but on my mention of Kelleher.

"What about her?"

"Look Ish, I don't much like her, but I'll do business with her if I have to."

He swallowed and put the sandwich back on the plate. He peeked over his shoulder and leaned forward, resting his forearms on the edge of the table.

"Stay away from her, Joth."

I leaned toward him as well, afraid of missing any nuance.

"I prefer to work with you…"

He shook his head vigorously.

"Stay away from her. She's trouble."

Ish's eyes were narrow and intensely focused, as if trying to communicate more than he could say in words.

"Dangerous?"

"Without a doubt."

I pushed back into the booth and stroked my chin.

"Okay. Thanks. Jimmie, does he…"

"He knows. I told him."

After this revelation, or perhaps because of it, Ish moved our discussion into the most banal territory he could muster. He even refused to talk about college football, which we both knew formed Jimmie's principal gambling book every autumn.

The conversation that ensued bored us both and it didn't take long for Ish to devour his lunch. He wiped his mouth with the red checkered napkin and got up. I followed him, paying and leaving a tip at the hostess stand. Outside, I held out my hand, but he turned away as if he hadn't noticed.

"See you, Ish."

"See you around."

Chapter Eight

The Hunter's Lodge in Daylight

Through the rest of that day and into the following morning, I considered confronting Kelleher. I didn't have much to go on, and she was too savvy and experienced not to see through one of my stunts. I wasn't even sure if, or how, the information Ish had delivered to Jimmie related to Hamburger's murder, but since Kelleher had been one of the first officers on the scene and because Jimmie's concern was tied to the party, the connection provided a good working assumption. So, I went back to the weakest link in the chain: The Great White Hunter, Tommy Kuhl.

The source of Kuhl's wealth was murky. His family had been at the forefront of massive resistance in the 50s and 60s and their reputation as a voice for what they called traditional values dated back even further. Tommy was the product of private schools, but he had washed out at two colleges. His father had found him a place in the family business where he could do no harm, and after the old man's death, Tommy had inherited both the hunting lodge where he now resided, and enough investment real estate to support his decadent lifestyle.

The fog of the morning had cleared, and the day had matured into a crystal clear, mid-autumn afternoon. Kuhl's windy country road shimmered with the reds, yellows and oranges of maples, tulip poplars and red oaks. I parked in the same spot Heather's Mustang had occupied the previous Saturday night.

Branching off from the familiar brick walkway was a flagstone path that led to the front door of the Tudor-style mansion. Above a fieldstone foundation, the walls were tan stucco crossed with heavy timber beams, studded with iron fixtures. I dropped the lion's head door knocker against the heavy oak door and stepped back. As I did, I noticed a lithe form fluttering behind a trio of casement windows with diamond panes on the second floor above the doorway. A moment later, this vision in flowing white opened the door. It was the girl who'd called herself Puck at the party, and except for the absence of faux wings, her appearance had hardly changed, right down to the glitter in her hair. It took me a moment to recover.

"Hello. I'm here to see Mr. Kuhl."

She stared at me as if she was waiting for the punchline. Before either of us could speak again, Tommy appeared behind her.

"Here now, Jenny, don't you have some chores to do?"

She agreed that she did and disappeared with the same weightless strides I remembered from Tommy's party. I looked at him and waited.

"Jenny's staying with me for a while."

I said nothing and he continued.

"She's my niece. I'm trying to get her back on her feet."

Jenny, or Puck, had thrown the door wide open, but Tommy pushed it partially shut and stood in the opening as if he were determined to bar my entry.

"I was hoping to talk to you about the party. Do you have a few minutes?"

"What about it?"

"I'm just trying to put the pieces together."

"You represent me on this. You said you would."

"I don't think you need a lawyer, Tommy. Besides, I'm just here to find out what happened."

"But you'll represent me if I need you, right? I mean, what we say is confidential, right?"

"Sure. Sure. Can I come in?"

With a shrug, he held the door open, then led me back to the same paneled room adorned with trophy heads where we had spoken on Saturday night. We took the same two chairs on opposite sides of the fireplace.

"Drink? Jenny can get us something."

I didn't want anything, but my curiosity demanded another look at Jenny.

"Sure, what are you having?"

"Apple cider. You can have it cold or warm."

It seemed a little early in the season for hot drinks.

"Cold will be fine."

He smiled and nodded, then called out Jenny's name. She appeared so quickly that she must have been lurking in the hallway. Tommy noticed the same thing and directed a sharp expression at her.

"Jenny, could you bring two cold ciders for myself and my friend?"

She absorbed the message, nodded, and flitted out of the room.

I was curious enough to venture an indiscrete question.

"How long have you had Jenny with you?"

A look of indignation flashed across his features, but it was a question he felt he needed to answer.

"She's my niece. I told you that. I'm caring for her while her parents are away."

"Your sister's kid?"

He hesitated.

"Yes."

He could see that I regarded this as fiction, and he tried again.

"Fact is, she left home and was working at one of those strip joints. Can you imagine? A girl as innocent as her? When I found out, I pulled her out of there, and here she is. Temporarily, of course."

His eyes shifted abruptly to the fireplace. I didn't believe him for a minute, so I mentally added sexual perversion to his known vices and moved on.

"There was an officer here Saturday night. A female officer. Dark haired? Attractive?"

He nodded.

"Kelleher. I spoke to her."

"That's her."

He winced at the memory and his expression grew somber.

"She was the first on the scene as far as I could tell," he said.

"She was probably in the closest squad car when the call went out. Do you know who called the police?"

"No idea. The news spread quickly, and people have cell phones."

He shrugged. It was a non-issue to him, and he had no additional information for me.

Jenny came in with the ciders, served in chilled copper mugs and smelling of cinnamon and cloves. She peered at me closely as she handed me mine, as if she thought she could read my intentions on my face. It was unnerving.

"Thank you, Jenny."

"Puck."

Tommy waited for her to leave.

"It's a little affectation, this Puck business. She has aspirations for the theatre."

"I can see that."

"I'm trying to help her."

I sipped my cider and considered his answer.

"Is she in school around here?"

"Not currently. No."

He took a long sip.

"What else can I help you with?"

He was defensive about Puck, but also about what had happened at his home on Saturday night. He had invited me in because he needed an ally, somebody to take his side.

"Tommy, if you want me to represent you, you're going to have to level with me."

"About what?"

"Let's turn back to Officer Kelleher. Can you remember anything she said? Any questions she asked?"

"She asked about the prosecutor, Mrs. Burke. I talked with her and with you, so I knew she was here and what she wore."

"Kelleher asked you about that?"

"Yes. She wanted to know what time she arrived."

"What did you tell her?"

"That I didn't know."

"Anything else?"

"Nothing I can think of."

I prodded him again. There was more, but nothing of significance. I asked the sort of by-the-book questions an investigating officer should ask. The only answers that disturbed me were the ones that linked Heather and Kelleher, but that may have been because Ish had fired up my suspicious mind.

"Alright. Thanks, Tommy."

I gave him a business card and he reciprocated by air dropping me his cell number.

"I can let myself out."

He nodded and didn't make a move to get out of his chair.

The house was constructed around a two-floor atrium with open hallways around the second level. As I made my way toward the front door, I heard the swish of diaphanous cloth. Jenny was tracking my movements from the second level.

Chapter Nine

A Visit with Irish Dan

There was only one strip joint in Arlington, a gentlemen's club in Crystal City, called Riding Time. I was always happy to make the drive to South Arlington because the proprietor, Irish Dan Crowley, was one of my closest friends and best sources of business.

It was mid-afternoon when I arrived. The lunch crowd had returned to work and Dan liked to use that time slot to give the new hires a chance to show what they could do or to hone their routines.

I spotted him behind the bar at the back of the long, low-ceilinged room, instructing a tall, broad-shouldered dancer in a red negligee who had her back to me. She was seated on a stool across the bar from Dan.

The backbeat pulsed loudly as I crossed a floor already sticky with spilled beer, a smell that lingered like cigar smoke. When Dan saw me, he dried his beefy hands with a bar towel and shooed away the young dancer. He came out from behind the bar and shook my hand.

Dan was a big man about my age. He made no effort to take care of himself and cared little for his personal appearance, but that all added up to a man without pretension. He wore an untucked plaid flannel shirt that was clean but wrinkled. I knew that he beamed the same warm smile to everyone who came into his place, but he always made me feel like I was his most important customer. I also knew I was one of the few people he considered a friend.

"Joth! Last time I saw you…"

"Yeah, that was then."

"Okay. Beer or coffee?"

"Coffee."

Bushy eyebrows bobbed above his pale blue eyes. He gave the order to a heavy-set woman with tattoos down both arms, who I knew as Q-tip.

"Let's get a booth."

We slid into one toward the back, where the pounding music and claustrophobic air were less oppressive. He folded his hands on the table.

"First of all, Dan, how've you been?"

"Good. Fall's always a good season for me."

He cocked his head and looked at me shrewdly.

"But you didn't come all the way down here to make small talk."

"You're right. I need something."

"Information?"

"That's usually it, isn't it?"

He opened his hands.

"I'll do what I can."

"It's about a young woman who used to work in a gentleman's club around here. Don't know much about her."

"Got a name?"

I was about to say Jenny, but that name felt like a sham. All of Dan's dancers got fitted with odd trade names, so I tried that.

"She calls herself Puck."

He thought about it and nodded.

"I had girl in here this summer who called herself Puck. Character from a book, I think."

"What can you tell me about her?"

He filled his cheeks and blew out his breath. I could tell by the way he furrowed his brow that the name made him uncomfortable.

"She was a runaway, as far as I could tell. Pretty girl. Thin, with a pasty complexion. Everything she wore was white. I don't think she would have lasted long."

A runaway! This didn't surprise me. I made a note to be suspicious if Kuhl told me that water was wet.

"What happened to her?"

"I don't know. She left one night and didn't come back. Didn't even pick up her last paycheck. Girl like that, well, it didn't surprise me."

"How old was she?"

Dan looked at me like he was offended by the question.

"Over eighteen."

"You sure?"

"Yeah, counsellor, I'm sure. I got a picture of her driver's license."

"Can I see it?"

He folded his arms actress his chest.

"What for?"

"This isn't about you, Dan. It's about her."

He looked at me for a long moment, then nodded. We'd been through a lot together and I don't think there was anyone he trusted more than me.

"Come on back," he said.

Dan's office was in a windowless cubbyhole behind the bar. The air was stuffy, and the furniture consisted of a wooden desk and chair and two armchairs that had probably graced the office of a mid-level government manager ten years before. I took one of the chairs and he began fiddling around in the cardboard boxes that constituted his filing system. After a few moments, he pulled out a Redwell with four thin file folders inside of it. One of these read "Jennifer Wren / Puck" on the flap. So, her name really was Jenny. He pushed the file across to me.

"Here you go. You can look at it here if you don't mind."

Inside, I found her employment eligibility verification form and a picture of her driver's license. The license showed a typical, unposed headshot. It wasn't much, but it was everything I needed.

She'd given an address in Williamsburg as her residence. She'd turned 18 in July, just a month before she started working for Dan. This and the out of the area address were probably why he had pegged her as a runaway. Perhaps he'd dropped that to Kuhl one night and didn't remember doing it. Once Kuhl latched on to her, he could have come up with the tall tale about the sister.

Inside the Redwell was an unopened payroll envelope, stamped and addressed to "Jenny Wren" at the Williamsburg address. It had been stamped "Return to Sender Addressee Unknown" by the post office.

"Her last paycheck?"

"Yup."

"She never came back for it?"

"No. It's not much. They mostly work for tips."

"Yeah, I know," I said.

I let my eyes wander to the ceiling while I considered what I'd found.

"Puck. How come you gave her a nickname when she came with an obvious one? You could have called her Wren."

"Puck was how she introduced herself when she came here. Kind of a wifty kid. I hope she's not in trouble."

"She might be. But not because of anything you did."

"You gonna get her back to her parents?"

I saw his Adam's apple bob. He smelled trouble.

"No. Nothing like that. She's a witness to something I'm working on. Is there anyone who might know where she went?"

"I'm not sure. She wasn't here long."

"A roommate, maybe?"

"I put her in an apartment with another girl I've got working for me."

"Can I talk to her?"

"I can check."

I tilted my head. There were two Dan's: the frank, open Dan I usually dealt with, and the canny, suspicious Dan. The first was his default persona. The appearance of the second always caught my attention.

"Check? Check what?"

"If she still works here."

He knew if she still worked for him.

"I'd appreciate it."

I shifted my weight to suggest a new topic, although it really wasn't.

"You know a guy named Kuhl? Tommy Kuhl? Maybe five-foot-nine, Blonde hair, long in the back and thinning on top. Calls himself the Great White Hunter."

He thought about it and shook his head.

"He'd be just another kook in this place."

Without asking, I used my phone to photograph Jenny Wren's I-9 and the driver's license. Dan didn't object. Then I got up and shook his hand.

"Anything else you can tell me about this Puck?"

"Well, she liked to dance. And like I said, a pretty girl, and not shy, but she didn't get it. She took her clothes off like there was no one else in the room."

I picked up the payroll envelope.

"I know where she lives. You want me to deliver the check?"

He seemed startled, but I had surprised Dan more times than he could count.

"Sure. It's her money."

As we walked together through the noisy, beery room, the smile returned to Dan's face. This was his domain and he loved it.

"About the roommate? You'll let me know?"

Friend in the Bullseye

"Yes, Sir."

"Thanks, Dan. I'll keep you posted."

Chapter Ten

The Brewer of Mischief

I kept my ear to the ground through my connections with court personnel and the media, and through with my alliances with people employed in law enforcement. TV, radio, and the papers treated Hamburger's murder like it was the only story in town, so it wasn't hard to pick up rumors, hints, and suggestions, but facts were elusive.

With no apparent progress to announce, I could sense the pressure on Heather's office growing. I heard whispers of it between lawyers at lunch and in the hallways of the courthouse. Some of these professed concern about rising crime in the county and many were willing to ride that tide for personal gain. Press and public interest groups wanted answers, but the police and the CA's office had none to offer. The first indication that the ice was breaking was a telephone call I got from someone named Missy Brewer.

Marie announced the call with a hushed gravity that struck me as odd. I picked up the receiver.

"Joth Proctor," I said.

"Hello Mr. Proctor. This is Missy Brewer."

Friend in the Bullseye

The cheery recitation of the caller's name made me think I should have recognized it. She had the husky voice of a lifetime smoker, but the name meant nothing to me.

"Good morning, Ms. Brewer. What can I do for you?"

I heard a brief laugh.

"I was told I might need a lawyer and that you're a good one."

"I'm sorry about that, but I hope I can help. What seems to be the trouble?"

"Well, it's that death last week. The man who was running for Commonwealth's Attorney?"

That got me to the edge of my chair.

"Randy Hamburger?"

"Yes. Well, the police have been around, asking some questions."

"I see. What kind of questions?"

"Like where I was when he was killed."

I'd already heard enough.

"Is there a time when you can come in and talk about it?"

"No time like the present."

I took a quick look at my calendar, though I knew there was nothing on it.

"Can you be here in half an hour?"

"Of course."

I gave her directions and told her where to park.

"See you in half an hour."

Missy Brewer arrived an hour and a half later, breezing in without apology. I stood up as Marie ushered her in. I gave Marie a courteous nod and offered Ms. Brewer one of the client chairs opposite my desk. She sat down and crossed her rather elegant legs.

She was pretty and alluring with large, wide-open eyes that gave her a perpetual expression of surprise. I pegged her age as 35. She was about 5' 5" and slim, with dirty blonde hair and the kind of clear complexion and even features that aged well.

"Do you mind if I smoke?"

My usual answer was "yes, I do," or sometimes, "the landlord objects," if client relations required a tactful refusal, but she was already shaking one out from a pack of Lucky's. She lit it and looked around for an ash tray. I handed her a dirty coffee mug with the blindfolded Lady Justice holding the scales on one side, but she missed the hint. She struck me as someone who might be immune to hints. I waited her out.

She blew a smoke ring at the ceiling.

"I got a visit from the police yesterday."

I took a heavy breath for affect.

"What did they want?"

"They wanted to know what I was doing last Saturday night."

"Which was?"

"I was home. Alone."

"You weren't at the party?"

"I just said that."

I nodded. That likely meant no alibi, but there might be neighbors or delivery people who had seen her. I made a mental note to ask DP to find out.

Missy spoke in crisp, professional tones, enunciating each syllable. She fidgeted, and I assumed she was anxious, but people facing a possible felony charge often are when meeting with a lawyer for the first time. She kicked at the edge of the carpet with the toe of her boot, and I knew she was considering whether to tell me something else.

I gave her the time she needed.

"My show is rough. That's what the sponsors want. Rough, provocative talk. I don't apologize for it."

"That's the business you're in?"

She tilted her head, looking at me as if I'd said something she didn't understand.

"Yes. It's a radio show."

"And what about this rough talk?"

"His name came up. Randy's name."

"You talk about him as if you know him."

She looked out the window for a long moment.

"I do."

She made a throw-away gesture with the hand holding the cigarette.

"I did."

"How did you know him?"

"I met him in law school."

"You're a lawyer?"

"No. I left law school for broadcasting. But that's where I met him."

"Broadcasting?'

"I wasn't happy in law school. Radio is the right place for me."

"So, you dropped out?"

"That's right."

I tried to recall where Hamburger had gone to school. George Mason law school was about two miles down Wilson Boulevard from where we were sitting.

"GMU?"

"That's right."

"That doesn't explain why the police are interested in you."

She shrugged.

"I don't get it either. He was running for office, so naturally we talked about that on the air. I may have said some things that weren't diplomatic."

"Such as?"

"It's just talk, you know. But I may have said something like, 'he's not fit to be Commonwealth Attorney.'"

Something like?

I let her watch me process this.

"Anything else?"

"No, just that one comment. It was stupid."

"Is that exactly what you said?"

Her eyes flashed.

"Probably."

I nodded, but I figured that meant no. I'd get the truth when she was ready to tell it.

"How well did you know Hamburger?"

"Well enough not to trust him."

That may have meant nothing more than she had discerning judgment about people.

"What would cause you to say something like that?"

She took a deep drag, tilted her head back, and exhaled slowly.

"He was a son of a bitch when I knew him. Ruthless."

That didn't mean much either. He was a son of a bitch on the day he died. She took another long drag.

"Sometimes, I talk too much, but it's hard not to. You have to fill the air, keep it going, keep ratcheting up the energy. The dead air gets filled, sometimes with things you wish you could take back."

"Did you oppose him politically?"

"I liked him politically. He was pro-church and anti all that LGBT foolishness. The one we have now is too soft on crime."

"I'm not sure I understand the source of your hostility toward him."

She put her hands on the arms of the chair with the attitude of someone who'd reached a clear decision.

"He accused a friend of mine of cheating in law school."

"Was he?"

"She. And no, of course not."

"How do you know?"

"Because he was the one who was cheating."

Now, it was my turn to straighten up in my chair.

"Randy Hamburger cheated on a law school exam?"

"Yes! And probably more than one."

"What happened to your friend?'

"She was forced to withdraw."

"You were close to this woman?"

She hesitated.

"Yes, very. It broke my heart."

"When's the last time you saw Hamburger?"

She took another long drag on the Lucky.

"I haven't seen him since I left school."

I waited, but she seemed drained. I'd gotten enough for the first day.

"Alright. I'm following this investigation closely and I haven't heard your name come up. Let me make some inquiries and see if you're on anyone's radar. We'll talk again. Is there anything else I should know?"

She shook her head.

There were a few administrative details to tie down. I told her that I needed a $10,000 retainer. It's the money question that usually raises eyebrows, but she was as unconcerned as if I'd asked her about the weather. I attempted casual conversation while I gathered intake information, but she had lost interest.

As I stood up, she ground the cigarette out in the coffee mug and handed it back to me.

"I'll have my assistant send you a representation agreement."

I walked Missy to the outer office door and watched as she climbed into a silver Jaguar parked in a handicapped spot out front. I'd seen no indication of a physical limitation, and her car lacked a handicap plate or sticker.

"I wonder how she affords those wheels on the salary of a radio personality."

Marie stopped typing and looked up at me.

"You don't know who she is, do you?"

"I guess I don't."

"That's Missy Brewer."

"So?"

"You need to get out more, Joth."

I looked at her inquiringly, waiting for the rest of it.

"She's known as 'The Brewer of Mischief.' She's got the most highly rated political talk show on the radio. And the mouth on her!"

Chapter Eleven

What's Crisp?

Dan called my office the following morning.

"Crisp will talk to you, but she wants it to be here."

"Who's Crisp?"

"Crisp is the name of the girl who used to live with Puck."

"Okay. When can I catch her?"

Many of Dan's girls were careful about the company they kept, and those who weren't often lived to regret it, but I was a known commodity and universally recognized around The Place, as it was known among the staff. Generally, the girls were willing to accommodate me with their time.

"She's got the afternoon shift today. How about four?"

"That's a busy, noisy time, Dan. Can she do something earlier?"

"You're lucky she's agreeing at all."

I picked up a hint of aggression in his tone.

"Sounds like she's hiding something."

"I'll see you around four, Joth."

I was at the bar at 3:45, enjoying a draft beer and chatting with Q-tip, Dan's floor manager and staff enforcer. For years, Dan had enjoyed a long and profitable business relationship with an older woman named Christine Barkley. Barkley handled the girls and the books with a grace and skill Dan had never mastered. Q-tip had assumed an increasingly prominent role in Dan's operation, and I guessed he was grooming her for the Mama Barkley post. If so, I needed to get to know her and bank some credibility. I talked to her about the business, while steering scrupulously clear of anything that might be considered snooping, a limitation I find hard to impose on myself. A question about beer suppliers hung in the air when a woman with dark hair and dressed in a scarlet negligee sat down on the stool beside me.

"Dan said you wanted to talk to me."

I turned to get a better look. She was tall and thin with disproportionally broad shoulders, and there was something unsettling about her appearance.

"Hello. Are you Crisp?"

"I am Crisp."

She spoke with an odd falsetto pluck to her voice and her large, meaty hands went to her face and hair as if she were making last minute adjustments to her appearance.

"Well, I'm Joth Proctor…"

"I know who you are."

She pressed a hand into her black, course hair.

"I'm glad to meet you. I understand you roomed with a girl who called herself Puck."

Crisp scowled.

"She didn't *call* herself that. That was her name. Just like I'm Crisp."

I took a more careful look at her, then broke eye contact when she blushed. There was an opaque, translucent quality to the skin on her cheekbones and her eyebrows were unnaturally high. This woman had been in an accident and the surgical repairs and plastic surgery had left their mark. Riding Time was an odd place to seek a new start, but Dan's generosity of spirit often surprised me. I tried to put her appearance out of my mind.

"What can you tell me about Puck?"

"Why do you want to know?"

"I'm trying to help her."

"Help her with what?"

Many of Dan's girls were cut from the same mold: pugnacious, defensive, and suspicious, but Crisp had an edge of hostility I wasn't used to.

"I know she's been in a little bit of trouble. I want to keep her from getting into more."

She pursed her lips.

"What do you care?"

I tried to gauge whether she was suspicious of my intentions or protective of Puck. Dan's girls typically looked out for each other, and some enjoyed the mother hen role. I guessed that Crisp was one of these.

"Sometimes, I'm able to make a difference. Dan will tell you that."

"You keep away from her."

"Did something bad happen? With Puck, I mean?"

Her face flushed again.

"What's in it for you?"

This was going nowhere. On an impulse, I put my cards on the table. Or at least most of them.

"I know the guy she ran off with and I don't like him."

"Which guy?"

"Tommy Kuhl."

Crisp had been speaking with increased animation, edging her elbows onto the bar as she did, but now she relaxed back onto the stool.

"I know Tommy Kuhl," she said.

"You've met him?"

She nodded, and when she spoke again, her tone had softened.

"Me and Puck, we worked the afternoon shift that day. I saw her talking to him in a booth during her break. That's not unusual. That's how we make our living."

"Then you never saw her again?"

"I came back to the apartment late that night and she was just leaving."

"With Tommy?"

"Yes. He helped her pack up. She didn't have much."

"Did you hear any of their conversation?"

She thought about it and lied.

"No."

"Did she go voluntarily?"

She hesitated.

"Yes."

"Are you sure?"

"She didn't have any other place to go."

"She could have gone home."

She sneered at me, as if I'd given away the game.

"You don't know her at all, do you?"

With the air of someone who had said more than she intended, she swiveled off the stool and walked away.

I still had a half-full beer in front of me and decided to enjoy the rest of it, hoping Crisp would rethink her bitter reaction and return. She didn't, but Dan did. He sat down on the vacant stool, poured my beer into the sink, and asked Q-tip to draw me a cold one.

"Did you get want you were after?"

"Nope."

"She's a hard case, but she's getting better."

"She's a little different than most of your girls. Was she in a bad car crash?"

"No."

"But the plastic surgery…"

Dan cocked his head and waited for me to think it through. It took a minute, but I figured it out.

"Oh."

"Crisp's legal name is Christine Kelly, but she was born Chester Kelly."

"I see."

He looked up and asked Q-tip for a beer, something he rarely did.

"Yeah. You know, she was up front about it, very committed that this was what she wanted. And she's good. Under the stage lights, she looks like any other slim, fit girl with silicone hooters."

"She seems kind of angry."

"I think it's fair to say that she hates men."

"Men in general?"

"Oh, she's had a couple of run-ins with intolerant patrons. I had to run a guy out of here last week who made rude comments to her. I thought she was going to kill him."

"She looks capable."

"I don't know. She's just trying to find her place in this world."

"So, she started life as a man?"

"She was born a male, but she was never a man. You know what I mean?"

I wasn't sure, and Dan saw the confusion on my face.

"She had a dick but didn't know how to use it. Well, some things, sure, but when it came to acting like a real man, she couldn't because she was really a woman all along. So, there were years of pretending. She fooled a lot of people, but she couldn't fool herself. That's what she told me. And finally, she faced up to who she really is."

"And you gave her a job."

"Sure. I hope she finds herself."

"That's a hell of a story."

"I hope it gets better."

I finished my beer, pushed the empty mug away and reached for my wallet.

"No charge."

"Thanks, Dan."

I stood up.

"Why don't you come around tomorrow? She'll be in a better mood once she's had a chance to think things through. That's always how it is with her. Crisp's a little emotional."

But I was already on to something else.

"What about this guy, Kuhl? The guy Puck left with? You said you didn't know him. Does this bring anything back?"

Dan shrugged his heavy shoulders.

"I probably met him, but that's what I do. I try to meet everyone."

"You wouldn't have said anything to Kuhl about Puck?"

He flashed an expression of disgust.

"No offense, Dan, but he might have asked a simple question, and you might have answered it. Look, this Kuhl may be a predator, and those people are slick."

He nodded. His commitment to his girls didn't end when they left his employ.

"What are you going to do, Joth?"

"I'm going to go to that Bavarian castle he lives in and get that girl the hell out of there."

On the drive back from Crystal City, I tried to let the emerging fall colors sooth me as I considered and rejected a half dozen possible ways to approach Kuhl. Then, I remembered Puck's final paycheck. The envelope was still in the pocket of my sport coat. I had promised Irish Dan that I would deliver it. Now, that promise would be redeemed.

Kuhl's garage doors were open and there were two cars inside: a late model Land Rover and a BMW coupe that looked like it had a lot of hard miles on it. I assumed that neither vehicle belonged to Puck, which made it likely that Kuhl was home. It was hard to tell about the girl.

I banged loudly on the brass knocker, then banged again on the door. I was willing to wait all afternoon, but it didn't take that long. Kuhl opened the door a crack and peered out.

"Yes, Mr. Proctor. What can I do for you?"

He spoke in an even voice edged with a note of exasperation.

I smiled and held up the Riding Times envelope.

"I know the proprietor over at Riding Time. The place where you found Jenny? This is her final paycheck. He asked me to give it to her."

The mention of Riding Time and my knowledge of his connection to it startled him.

"I'll take it."

He reached for it with a gesture of impatience and an air of ownership that offended me. I snatched it back.

"Dan told me to give it to her personally."

"Well, she's not here."

"I'll come back.'"

"Just drop it in the mail."

He shut the door in my face.

I backed away a step, and as I did, I thought I saw a wispy figure move behind the casement windows above the door. I looked up and saw Jenny Wren in what looked to be a white bathrobe flowing loosely around her. She was gazing down at me with an expression I couldn't read in the glare reflecting on the windows, but I believed I saw a pleading look on those pale features, like a bird in a diamond-paned cage.

I'd had about enough of Mister Thomas Kuhl.

Chapter Twelve

Unlocking the Puzzle

My landlord and sometimes collaborator, DP Tran, ran a private detective agency from his office on the second floor of his two-story cinderblock office building near the courthouse. DP was also a bail bondsman and locksmith, and if the price was right, he'd shape-shift into whatever other professional you needed him to be.

I went up to ask if he'd made any progress on a matter of personal importance to me: locating my long-missing father. I found DP at the worktable that occupied the center of the long room. He was disassembling the kind of lock you might find on the door of a house you were trying to break into. At least that's what I thought when I saw what he was doing.

"I don't want to know what you're up to."

"You're better off that way."

He grinned without showing his uneven teeth. DP was small and fit as a jockey, with a perpetually inquisitive look on his round face. When I asked him about my father, he grimaced and shook his shaven head.

"I ran him through all the sources and databases I've got. You got anything else to go on?"

"The family bible wasn't enough?"

"You gave me everything you typically need: birthdate, social security number, past addresses. I ran all that stuff and more. No trace of him. It's as if he disappeared from the Earth in 1990. I know he'll resurface, but it's almost like he doesn't exist."

DP took a careful look at me and nodded. He was thorough and he didn't like to fail, and he knew how important this was to me.

"Well, keep at it, will you?"

"You know I will. By the way, was somebody smoking in your office yesterday?"

I was angry at myself, not so much for letting Missy break one of DP's hard and fast rules, but for failing to immediately clear the air with my landlord after it happened. For a guy who operated a below-market office space without amenities, he could be awfully prickly about some things.

"Sorry. I was going to tell you."

"How did it happen?"

I shrugged, stumbling to find language he might respond to.

"Pushy broad. She had it lit before I knew what she was doing."

"Is she coming back?"

"Well, she hired me, so I guess she is."

"It won't happen again, will it?"

I considered the prospect of her return and her apparent unwillingness to comply with the rules of others.

"I'll see that it doesn't."

"I feel better already."

I sat down across from him as another thought occurred to me.

"You ever heard of a woman named Missy Brewer?"

DP had been anxiously twirling a pen in his right hand. Now, he put it down.

"The Brewer of Mischief?"

"That's what Marie called her. Is that supposed to mean something?"

"It does if you actually have a life. She's a talk show host."

"That's what she said."

"She's a muckraker, a name caller, and a rabble rouser."

"What do you really think about her?"

"If I ever see her, I'll tell her to her face. Whatever she's tied up in must be ugly."

DP was usually more circumspect. I suspected he was trying to avoid whatever salacious details I had.

"It is. Don't get too upset with her. She might need you."

"This has got to do with Hamburger, doesn't it?"

"What makes you think that?"

"Come on. She threatened to kill him on the air."

That caught my attention.

"You listen to her show?"

"Sometimes."

"What did she say about him?"

"I'll bet it was different from what she told you."

"It wouldn't be the first time. Come on, give."

He shrugged his narrow shoulders.

"Something like, 'He's not only not fit to be Commonwealth's attorney; he's not fit to be alive.'"

I whistled. That was quite a bit different from what she'd told me.

"Did it sound like an actual threat to you?"

"Sure. But they don't call it a talk show for nothing. She's in the entertainment business, not politics. Although if it got her in trouble, I wouldn't complain."

"She told me Hamburger accused a friend of hers of cheating in law school. Got the woman expelled."

"That would be a good reason to hate him."

"This was at George Mason, maybe a dozen years ago. Can you find out what happened?"

"That's a pretty tall order. The trail's pretty cold."

"But you'll do it, right?"

"Of course. What else you need?"

I laughed.

"I'd like to know who killed Randy Hamburger."

"Is someone going to pay me for this?"

"I've got a client. She's good for it."

"Missy Brewer? Or is it Heather?"

"What makes you think that?"

"Scuttlebutt."

DP was a magnet for courthouse gossip.

"That's still an open question."

DP chuckled. Ethical niceties rarely concerned him. He was only interested in answers, and I knew we could operate on that basis.

"Okay. I'll poke around. Anything else?"

I had a vague recollection of a murder prosecution from several years back when the victim died of strychnine poisoning. A wealthy man was found dead by his pool. The tool shed was unlocked. Apparently, the strychnine had been used to kill rats. I told DP what I could remember, which wasn't much. As usual, he didn't disappoint. He remembered it right away.

"Yeah, a case called Luigi."

"DP, you are a walking compendium of Arlington criminal law."

"What do you want to know?"

"There aren't a lot of places where you can find enough strychnine to kill a person, even a little rat like Hamburger. I'd like to know where the poison that killed Luigi came from. Maybe the poison that killed Hamburger came from the same place."

"Why don't you ask Heather?"

"I'd like to keep her out of this. Sue Crandall's running the case and it's already tense enough over there."

"I get it. The investigating officer was Frank Moran. You know him?"

That was a stroke of luck.

"Yeah, I do."

DP chuckled.

"He's usually easy to find around lunch time."

Chapter Thirteen

Manicotti with a Side of Strychnine

I walked over to the police barracks, where the duty officer told me something I didn't know: Moran had retired in August.

"I hadn't heard."

"Yeah, it was kinda sudden."

"Hope it's not a health issue."

The desk officer's name was McMillian. He looked at me probingly but ignored the inquiry.

"Anyway, I was hoping to grab him for lunch."

He checked his watch. Then, he looked at me with the air of a man trying to gauge how much to give away.

"He was just here, trying to find someone to have lunch with."

"Did he have any luck?"

"He's retired. No one has to have lunch with him anymore."

"Do you know where he's eating?"

"Il Radicchio. You know it?"

"Yeah."

"You can still catch him. I'm sure he'd be thrilled."

It was an easy walk, but I was pretty sure that's not how Moran got there. I walked the quarter mile and found him in a booth by himself. He looked up as I entered.

"Hey, Joth!"

He gave me a friendly wave but didn't get up as I walked over.

"Join me?"

"Don't mind if I do."

Frank Moran could be fairly described as a portly man, and like a lot of big men, he dressed in anachronistic elegance, right down to the black onyx cufflinks and the wine-colored silk tie he was protecting by tucking his napkin into his collar. His complexion was florid. He wore his graying hair long in the back and he had a neat, gray mustache.

"Frank, you eat more Italian food than any Italian I know."

He laughed.

"You must not know many Italians."

"How come you're eating alone?"

He eyed me carefully, then shrugged.

"As soon as you retire, you're forgotten. Maybe that's why so many people keep working past retirement age. They need someone to have lunch with."

"Well, today you've got me."

He chuckled and waved for the waiter. It wasn't crowded, and he responded quickly. Frank spoke up before I could.

"You like manicotti? My order's already in. We can order another and split them both when they come."

I agreed.

Frank rubbed his hands at the prospect.

"Sausage?"

"Sure."

He gestured to the waiter, who nodded.

"Drink?"

He had a cocktail glass in front of him with a slice of lemon floating in it.

"Just water for me."

"Well, that's settled."

I unwound a little.

"Last time I saw you was over at Riding Time."

"Riding Time?"

He chuckled.

"Must have been somebody else. My priest wouldn't approve."

I wasn't sure what he meant. Frank was unmarried. He pushed back from the table.

"What are you doing here?"

"Looking for someone."

"Yeah? Who's that?"

"You."

He laughed. Frank was easily amused, or at least he liked to give that impression. He was a tough nut who made a career of using his jovial personality to disarm those he investigated. I knew this, and he knew I knew it, so he dropped the cheerful persona. He stroked his chin as I continued my probe.

"I hope you're keeping your hand in a little bit. You have any insight on what happened to Randy Hamburger?"

Frank emitted a burst of jovial laughter that struck me as incongruous with the subject of death.

"What do you want to know?"

"We could start with who killed him."

He studied me for a moment, then shrugged and looked away.

"Whoa, boy. That's the question everybody's asking."

"What's the answer?"

"Can't get me. I was in Ireland when it happened."

"Ireland!"

"A little retirement present to myself. Fifty-eight years old and I've never been."

"That surprises me."

"I hate planes. Always have. But I knew I had to get there before I go, and there's no time like the present."

"Did you know Hamburger?"

"Me? No, not really. But I liked him. Irish on his mother's side, you know. He was always telling me I needed to get back to the Auld Sod."

Frank's order arrived: a single tube of manicotti smothered in marinara sauce with two sausages. He cut the pasta in half with surgical precision and put half on my bread plate along with one sausage. He dug right in.

"Who you working for?"

"I'd rather not say."

"But you want me to cough it up?"

He shook his head vigorously.

"That doesn't seem right."

"A friend asked me to keep an eye on it."

As he chewed, Frank gave me the probing look I was used to and that I expected.

"That wouldn't be Ms. Burke, would it?"

That was a telling response, especially since DP had reached the same conclusion. I answered him carefully.

"She's a friend of mine. I'm here on behalf of a client."

He smirked. He had my answer, and he could draw whatever conclusion he liked.

"Okay, out with it. What do you want to know?"

"I want to know about strychnine."

He put his silverware down.

"Why you comin' to me?"

"Because you investigated a similar case a few years ago."

"So?"

"Luigi."

"Right. You thinking whoever killed Luigi might have killed Hamburger?"

"Nope. But I'm wondering if they got their poison from the same source."

"That's an idea."

"You got any thoughts on it?"

"Do I have any thoughts?"

He tapped his foot.

"Yeah, I've got some thoughts."

"You mind sharing them?"

Moran was a man who liked to talk. As a police investigator, he'd grown sensitive to the way his ideas were often dismissed by those more educated but less sensible than him, or so he had believed. I guessed it was one of the complaints that had led to his retirement.

"These are just thoughts, mind you."

"Your thoughts usually point in the right direction. That's all I'm looking for."

"I don't remember where the Luigi strychnine came from. In small quantities, it's not that hard to get. They use it to make rat poison."

"How much does it take to kill a person?"

"Not much. A few milligrams will do it. It's odorless. Got a very bitter taste. The guy who killed Luigi mixed it with cough syrup."

"How come they didn't get him?"

"Because the guy fled."

"So, the case is still open?"

He cleared his throat.

"Technically, yes. But I won't be around to nail the bastard if he ever turns up again."

"So, they know who did it?"

"I think so."

"In poison cases, it's usually someone who has professional access to it or stumbles on to it somehow," I said.

"That's right. In Luigi it was the gardener, though how that fits in with Hamburger, I don't know. Got anything else?"

"That's it."

"Where does that get you?"

"More confused than ever."

Frank chewed and nodded.

"You're way ahead of me."

"I doubt it."

He laughed, gratified that I was thinking along with him.

"You know what might help," I said. "The strychnine that killed Luigi is still in the evidence room. There's got to be some identifying details on the container."

"Manufacturer?"

"Or whoever had it in their inventory. Anyway, wouldn't that be a good place to start?"

"You can't get in the police evidence room."

"Oh, I can manage that."

Frank looked troubled.

"I'd forget that, Joth. That case is as cold as they come."

"You never know."

"I'd help you if I could, Joth, but I was in Ireland."

"I've heard it's beautiful."

"I got a cheap fare. I'm not getting any younger, you know."

"Sort of a bucket list item?"

He snapped his fingers.

"That's it! A bucket list item. Always wanted to go."

"I understand. Anyway: the evidence room. Heather can get in there."

"Yeah, I know. I'm not sure she should be getting her hands dirty, Joth."

I nodded.

"I see what you mean. People could draw the wrong conclusion. They often do."

Friend in the Bullseye

I drifted off into thought as Frank continued eating.

He was an engaging conversationalist when work was off the table. As he finished, he put his knife and fork down and asked about new restaurants and my reaction to the latest TV shows, my thoughts on the NFL and national politics. He listened to my brief and usually uninformed answers before launching a monologue on each topic.

Finally, he pushed his empty plate away.

I made my excuses and got up to leave.

"I hope I haven't wasted your time."

"No. This has been very helpful."

"You haven't touched your manicotti."

"You take it, Frank."

I put down $20 on the table. I wasn't paying for the manicotti. This was the ante for Frank's cooperation.

Chapter Fourteen

Coffee with Missy

On the walk back up the hill to my office, I wondered why Missy Brewer hadn't given me the full story surrounding the cheating incident. I was used to clients that didn't tell me everything, like a doctor who gets a slanted report of symptoms from a sick patient who fears the worst and hopes to wish the disease away. But if I was going to represent her, I needed all the facts, especially the ones that made her uncomfortable. A law school contretemps more than a decade old seemed like weak motivation to kill someone, but people have killed for much less. I didn't trust Missy, and I wanted to test her and flesh out her story.

Heather liked doing business at Willard's because its dim lighting, spartan design, and usually vacant tables created a forbidding atmosphere that tended to gin up the pressure on reluctant parties. It hadn't worked as well for me, but I thought it best to keep Missy and her Lucky's out of my office. Besides, I was willing to use whatever edge I could.

I called and asked to meet with her, and she responded with surly suspicion.

"Why?"

"Because I'm your lawyer and there are some things I need to understand."

"You said you'd look into it."

"I have been looking into it. That's why we need to talk."

That did it, as I thought it would. She didn't like the idea of anyone holding cards she couldn't see.

"We're having some work done in the office. You know a place called Willard's near the courthouse?"

She didn't, so I gave her the address.

"Can you be there in an hour?"

She hesitated.

"Is this really important?"

She was one of those people who felt that retaining a lawyer ought to insulate her from all legal inconveniences without further ado. I'd seen that before, too.

"Just be there."

"Alright."

That's when I found out something else about Missy. She responded when you pushed back.

I was crossing Wilson Boulevard when she roared up in her silver Porsche."

"Need a ride, Handsome?"

Nobody calls me that unless they have an ulterior motive. Her Porsche was blocking the travel lane and traffic was backing up behind her. I hopped in.

"You're punctual," I said.

"Does that surprise you?"

"Yeah, it does. Punctual people are usually courteous."

She screeched away from the curb, and we circled the block. I showed her where to park and watched the aggressive yet nimble way she worked the stick and clutch as she backed into a tight space.

Small, slim, fit, and exuding self-confidence, she was the sort of woman who became more attractive the more you saw of her. At least that's how she impressed me. But no one took notice of her as we walked toward Willard's.

"If you were on TV, you couldn't walk down this street without people flocking around for your autograph. Is that the next step for you?"

"TV? Hell no."

"Why not?"

"You just said it. I don't like to be noticed."

She drove a Porsche aggressively and wore a skirt so short it was hardly a skirt at all. She wasn't shy about being noticed. She just wanted to control who was doing the noticing.

We found a table inside. As Raighne made his way over to take our order, Missy rapped her pack of Lucky's on the table, ready to draw one out.

"You can't smoke here, Miss."

Missy didn't hesitate.

"Just watch me."

It looked like a clash of heavyweight wills was brewing. I took Missy by the wrist.

"It's a nice day. Let's go for a walk."

The Courthouse area was dotted with green spaces. One of them, across Wilson Boulevard, featured a bocce ball court and several cast iron tables with colorful umbrellas, each inserted through a hole in the center. No one was playing bocce, and the tables were empty. I selected the one with the least shade and left her the seat where the sun would illuminate her face. I also hoped the bright warmth would make her uncomfortable. Physical discomfort sometimes reveals hidden truths.

"I like this. It's almost like a date."

I tried to like my clients, and that was often difficult. I already didn't like Missy Brewer.

"Is there something you haven't told me?"

She tapped out the cigarette.

"About what?"

"About you and Randy Hamburger?"

She lit it and took a long drag.

"Look, the police are going to find out. I don't want to be the last one to know."

"I said something stupid on the radio. But that's my job. That's what I get paid to do."

"How many times have you threatened to kill someone in front of ten thousand listeners?"

A savage look came over her face.

"Ten thousand's a slow day."

"What did you say about Hamburger?"

"I said I owed him, and I'd get back at him."

"How well did you know him?"

"Somewhat."

"Were you friends?"

"He dated my roommate. He was interested in me, but I wouldn't go out with him."

"What was her name?"

"Phyllis. Phyllis Doyle."

"This Phyllis, was she your friend?"

"Yes."

"How did she meet Hamburger?"

"I don't know. I mean, the same way we all did. We were in school together."

"In other words, you don't want to tell me."

"That's right."

"What was the class he cheated in?"

"Constitutional Law."

She scowled at the memory.

"I said he'd get what's coming to him."

"That's not what you told me yesterday."

"It was a show about the local elections. I said I knew him well enough to distrust him."

"If that's all you said, we wouldn't be talking."

"The guest said something that pissed me off and I said I owed him, and I'd get him back. That's it."

"And you thought it would be better if I heard it first from the prosecutor?"

Missy didn't want to face a murder charge, but she also didn't want to appear foolish. At this moment, her reputation was perhaps more valuable to her than her freedom.

"I shouldn't have said it. Big deal."

"It could be a big deal in the hands of a sharp prosecutor. Especially if you can't keep your story straight."

I watched for her reaction to that threat, but she was a tough bird. I tried another approach.

"You don't seem to be bothered by the risk. Are you worried about losing your job?"

She laughed.

"Are you kidding? My producer would pay for that sort of notoriety. It'll boost advertising and ratings."

"Are you saying that's why you did it?"

"No, but the answer is yes if it'll help."

Missy had been in law school long enough to know she was offering to perjure herself, but maybe she'd forgotten.

"When did it happen?"

"About a month ago."

"Can you get me a tape? Of the whole show?"

"I'm sure I can."

"I'd like to know a little more about this cheating incident back in law school."

"What does it matter?"

"The police are going to think it does."

"Alright."

She took a long drag and tilted her head back to release it.

"Randy was at the top of the class, and he had his hand out for the brass ring: a federal court clerkship, then a job with a big firm. He had every step of it mapped out. He wasn't going to let anything get in his way. He had a little trouble with Con Law and he got panicky about it. So, he cheated."

"And when things got hot, he blamed your friend."

"That's it."

I wondered when her story would stop changing. Most likely, she was waiting for me to guide her toward her best story. I felt sure she'd swear to anything I suggested.

"And there was no romantic entanglement between you two?"

"Of course not. Never gave him the time of day. That's why he hated me."

"He hated you because you wouldn't go out with him?"

"That's right."

"What's the name of the cop who spoke to you?"

"Kelleher. Something Kelleher."

That would be Christine Kelleher, who was the first cop on the murder scene *and* the person Ish McGriff had warned me about. By now, I had concluded that Christine had turned on Jimmie, and that's what had made Jimmie edgy at our last meeting, but that was an issue for another day.

Missy pulled a business card out of the flap pocket in her blue blazer and looked at it.

"Christine Kelleher."

She handed me the card. I glanced at it and gave it back to her.

"You can keep it," she said.

"I know where to find her."

"You know her?"

"A little bit."

We fenced around the subject for a few more minutes. Then, I stood up to stretch.

"That's enough for today," I said. "Let me talk to Kelleher."

"Okay. Can I give you a ride back?"

We were closer to my office than we were to her car, and she knew it. This wasn't a joke, and it wasn't a come on. It was an effort to manipulate me. I was pretty confident that she treated most men this way.

"I can make it from here."

She nodded as she got up.

"And Missy? Get me that tape."

Chapter Fifteen

New Sheriff in Town

I needed to look at the strychnine being held in the evidence room. Beyond that, there wasn't much to do for Missy other than monitoring activity in the police and prosecutors' offices. Asking too many questions risked raising her profile among the investigative authorities. Yet, the police had approached her, and I would be remiss if I didn't try to get my hands around the status of the investigation and her place in it.

There was a new sheriff in town, almost literally. I'd gotten spoiled working with a prosecutor who was also a trusted friend. Calls were returned promptly, and although Heather and I sometimes battled like gladiators, we both knew the other could always be trusted. The first inkling I got of the new paradigm was the time it took for Crandall to return my call. On the third day after I'd left a message, Marie announced her over the intercom.

"Hi Sue. Congratulations on getting this assignment."

"Cut the crap, Joth. I've got a lot of calls to return."

"Okay. I've been retained in the Hamburger case."

"Kuhl?"

"I beg your pardon?"

I thought she said "cool" and that did not compute.

"Are you representing Tommy Kuhl?"

She sounded impatient.

"What makes you think that?"

"He says you are."

"Well, he's dealing with a lot of pressure."

"What kind of pressure?"

"Like a man who found a corpse in his backyard. That kind of pressure."

"And that makes him a suspect?"

I wasn't sure if that was a question or a statement.

"Sue, I didn't say anything about Tommy Kuhl. You brought him up."

"You spent a hell of a lot of time with him on the night of the murder. Kelleher said you implied that you represented him."

Word was traveling quickly.

There was an edge to Sue's voice that was unpleasant and personal. Heather never let the job get too big for her, but I wondered if Sue was in over her head.

"Kelleher jumps to too many conclusions."

"So, what are you wasting my time for?"

If this was a ploy to get me off my game, she was having some success, but I couldn't see how that would benefit Sue, who should have been using this call to gather all possible intel about my knowledge and purpose.

"I represent Melissa Brewer. She seems to think she's a suspect."

"She is."

"Based on what?"

"She had a grudge against Hamburger, and she threatened revenge. She didn't tell you that?"

If Heather had been running the show, I'd simply ask what she was talking about, but I needed to take a more combative and formalistic approach with Sue.

"That's never coming into evidence."

"She's got the most popular political talk show around. I've got my pick of thousands of possible witnesses who'll testify they heard it."

"It's talk radio, Sue. You're not supposed to believe what they say."

"That's for the jury to decide."

"You're pretty far along on this in a week."

"Hey, if you've got something I need to know, I'll listen."

"Look, I just want to see that justice is done, especially because I don't think that involves Ms. Brewer."

"Don't try to cozy up to me, Joth. Those days are over."

"What can you tell me about the poison?"

"It was strychnine."

"I know that. Where did it come from?"

"If you figure that out, I'll get you a conviction."

"Will you let me know if you find out?"

"Not likely, Joth. Not unless you've got something to trade."

"I'm just trying to find the killer."

"You're just trying to keep me from targeting your client…or clients."

After hanging up, I rubbed the heels of my hands into my eye sockets and pushed my hands back through my hair.

So, it wasn't Heather who'd latched on to Missy Brewer as a suspect. It was Sue Crandall. She had hit the ground running, already identifying someone with a long-standing grudge against the victim as a suspect.

I wondered how Crandall knew this. As a host of a weekday radio show, Missy was a public figure, but I was surprised Sue had made the connection so quickly. Perhaps it just showed that she was digging hard and knew where to dig. I wondered if Heather would approve, or if she'd feel threatened by her long-time deputy's mastery of the levers of power.

And then there was Christine Kelleher. I represented a suspect in a murder case and the prosecutor held a grudge against me. I had thought that Christine Kelleher did too, so I was surprised that she'd sent Missy my way. It was just common courtesy to thank her. A thank you call might also help me get a few more answers.

Chapter Sixteen

Off Limits

I was worried about Heather, so I decided to call on her first. It was a sparkling autumn morning as I crossed Courthouse Road, and the leaves along Wilson Boulevard showed brilliant autumn colors.

A chill in the morning air emboldened me. When in a hurry, feeling lazy, or particularly iconoclastic, I sometimes use the courthouse elevator marked "Police Elevator: Authorized Personnel Only" to cut through the security measures protecting the halls of justice.

I was not one to begrudge an appropriate level of security in a public building, but trivial inconveniences abounded in the courthouse. It seemed to me that the overriding point was not public safety, but to teach the citizenry to tremble before the awful capacity of the system to enforce its petty dictates.

My habit of casual disregard sometimes engendered raised eyebrows or impatient expressions. Since most cops and judicial employees didn't know who I was or if they did, they assumed Heather had granted me permission, I knew I could continue this mild indiscretion if I didn't push it or run into someone shrewd and experienced enough to recognize my game and call me on it. Someone like Christine Kelleher.

She entered the elevator on the second floor. She punched the fifth-floor button and glared at me.

"What are you doing on this elevator?"

"Hoping to run into you."

My quick response took her by surprise, as I hoped it would, and she scrambled to recapture her official poise.

"You know this elevator is off limits to civilians?"

"I must have missed the sign."

"I don't think so."

"Maybe I can buy you a cup of coffee and we can talk about it."

When the doors opened on the third floor, Kelleher was forced to step aside to make room for a pair of chatty deputy clerks. We both exited on the fifth floor, home to the office of the Commonwealth Attorney. When I saw that we were headed to the same place, I held the door for her. She pushed past me without thanks, turned left and entered a litigation war room without knocking.

I hadn't visited the CA's office since Hamburger's death. What I saw and heard when I stepped inside told me that the all-business vibe Heather had carefully cultivated over her term in office still prevailed. The place was buzzing like a beehive. Deputy prosecutors and staffers, papers in hand, cell phone at the ear or engaged in subdued conversations, marched purposefully back and forth across the deep, plush carpet. Printers and copiers whirred and telephones rang.

In the spacious reception area, floor to ceiling windows presented an awesome panorama of the nation's capital to the east. As I took in this familiar and still impressive scene, Betty, Heather's long-time assistant and gate keeper, looked up from her desk and smiled.

She stood up to greet me.

"You've been scarce around here, Joth."

I nodded toward Heather's closed door.

"I assume she's had a lot on her plate."

She pinched my elbow. Betty's tenure in the office predated Heather's, and though she was close to retirement age, she didn't look it. Her gray hair was cut short, and her posture remained ramrod straight, a picture of the brisk efficiency Heather relied on.

"That's when she needs you," she said. "You know that."

Betty did not dissemble, at least not when she dealt with me. She wouldn't tell me things she couldn't, and I knew better than to push her, but she'd tell me anything if she thought it could help Heather.

"Is she in?"

"I don't know where she is."

Her face clouded. She bobbed her eyebrows and her blue eyes seemed to lose some of their luster. This was unusual, and she knew I knew it.

"Normally, I'd let you go in and wait, but things are pretty crazy around here."

She said this with a quick nod toward the war room that Officer Kelleher had entered.

"I understand Sue's running with that Hamburger matter."

"Oh yes, she is. She's put her own team together and walled Heather off. That's what the statute requires, I guess, but she's been quite secretive. I can't get a thing out of her."

"Is she making any progress?"

"I assume so. People come and go—officers, detectives, assistants—all looking smug. She's gotten good at saying nothing while sounding self-important."

This was a trait quickly acquired by Commonwealth's Attorneys across the state who were bent on staying in office. Heather was a notable exception.

"And that group includes Christine Kelleher?"

"It does now."

"Now?"

"Heather had her taken off the street. Assigned her to the Evidence Room. Talk about a dead-end job. This

Hamburger investigation has been a career saver for Christine."

"I wonder how she pulled that off."

"How well do you know Officer Kelleher?"

I was about to say, "too well," but I demurred.

"I've run into her on a few cases."

"A difficult lady, isn't she?"

"She seems smarter than the average cop."

"Oh, she'll be the first to agree with that. When Sue took over this Hamburger mess, Kelleher practically begged Sue to get her out of the doghouse. I guess she convinced Sue that Heather had undervalued her."

That sounded like a savvy play. Sue would be predisposed to trust anyone distrusted by her predecessor.

I asked Betty to tell Heather I'd come by, which I knew she would do anyway, and our conversation veered toward friends and acquaintances we'd lost track off, but when I saw Kelleher exit the war room and head for the exit, I bade Betty a quick goodbye and followed.

Because I was aware she occasionally moonlighted for Jimmie Flambeau, Kelleher had reason to be suspicious of me. I caught up to her as she waited for the authorized personnel elevator to arrive. She didn't object when I followed her on. We were the only passengers.

"What's this all about?" she said.

"I thought we might talk."

"About what?"

"What happened to Randy Hamburger."

"And what do you know about that?"

"Not a damn thing, except that Missy Brewer didn't kill him."

"How do you know that?"

"You're right, I don't. But she says she didn't, and it will help her if I can find the person who did."

"Leave it to the police, Mr. Proctor. We don't need you mucking it up."

"The police sometimes make mistakes."

"Not this time."

"Sounds like you're pretty far along."

The doors opened on the first floor. She turned to walk away.

"Just stay out of the way."

"Look Chris, I've known you a long time…"

She spun back toward me.

"Not long enough to be calling me by my first name."

She'd done a nice job of recapturing the high ground. I took a long breath and started again.

"Okay. Forget it. Look, I know you were the first cop on the scene. I'd like to know what you turned up."

She measured me for a long moment. She was an attractive woman, if you liked the type: dark hair and strong features and a full, hard body. I tried not to think of that.

"Okay. Coffee."

There was a Starbucks on the other side of the parking lot. There was no line, and in keeping with department regulations, we each ordered and paid for our own coffee. The sparkling morning had developed into a bright and temperate autumn day. We found a table outside. She'd ordered something cold and was drinking it through a straw.

"First of all, thanks for referring Missy Brewer to me. It's a complement, and I appreciate it."

"She needed a good lawyer. I know that's you."

"How do you know her?"

"Our paths have crossed. What do you want to know, Joth?"

"As I said, you were the first cop on the scene…"

"I may have been the first, but that was a coincidence. I was in the area when the call came in, that's all."

"I know you scared the hell out of Tommy Kuhl."

I chuckled and we shared a laugh.

Christine Kelleher could be as strict and inflexible as a fundamentalist preacher, but she could slide into the coquetry at the blink of an eye. It was hard to ignore her clear, fine skin and strong features.

"He's a surprisingly nervous guy for someone with his reputation as a big game hunter. I thought you were going to represent him."

"I don't think he needs a lawyer. Do you?"

"As far as I'm concerned, everybody who was there needs a lawyer. Even you."

"I think I'll take my chances."

She leaned toward me to emphasize her words.

"Joth, this is a big-time, high-profile murder, and we're going to get whoever did it."

"And who do you think that is?"

She shrugged and broke eye contact. I answered my own question with another one.

"Who benefits?"

"Your girlfriend, Heather, for one. She wants to keep her job."

I wasn't surprised she thought this, as Heather's motive was self-evident, but I was shocked that she gave voice to it.

"Is that what you think?"

"I thought you were representing Brewer."

"No matter who I'm representing, I need to see as many cards as I can."

"Well, you're not going to see mine."

I processed that and veered to another approach.

"Heather has an open file policy. She gives defense attorneys access to everything she's got. I assume Sue will follow the same practice."

"There are guilty people walking the streets because of that policy."

"So, Sue's going back to trial by ambush?"

"I didn't say that."

"We all have the same goal. I'd like to know how Sue sees things and how she's going to approach this."

"Ask her. But she's not going to let the guilty walk because their lawyers got an early peek at the evidence."

I could see by her pursed lips and the heightened color on her face that she was growing angry. Christine realized it, too. She looked at her watch and got up abruptly.

"I've gotta go."

"Got a date?"

"As a matter of fact, I do."

"Lucky guy."

"Don't snow me, Joth."

I watched her go, feeling that I'd made progress. She'd called me by my first name.

Chapter Seventeen

DP Reports

Late that afternoon, DP knocked on my doorframe, a self-satisfied smile lighting up his sallow features. I put my pen down as he came in and sat down across from me.

"She fudged the story. Missy, I mean."

"I figured that."

"Some of what she said is true. For example, Hamburger had a reputation for being smart and ambitious. And there was a cheating incident in the Con Law class."

"Hamburger?"

"No. It was his girlfriend. Someone named Phyllis Doyle."

That was the name I'd gotten from Missy.

"What happened?"

He tapped the tip of an index finger against his nose.

"It's kind of fuzzy."

"Missy said Hamburger was the one who was cheating."

"If so, the school swept it under the carpet. It looks like Doyle was expelled or dropped out. Anyway, she didn't return in the fall," said DP. "But I'll tell you something interesting. Missy also left school over that summer."

"She told me she withdrew because she had the radio opportunity."

"Makes sense. At least it's consistent with what we know."

"Is there any reason to think those events are related?"

"Not yet."

"Do we know anything about Doyle?"

"Nothing right now. You want me to keep digging?"

Missy was a bit too entangled with Hamburger for my liking.

"Of course."

DP's information confirmed some of what Missy had told me, but the still-developing story contained several holes. Who was Phyllis Doyle? If Hamburger was cheating, how come Doyle paid the price? Was it a coincidence that Missy Brewer dropped out shortly thereafter?

"What grade did Missy get in Constitutional Law?"

"That's the funny thing. She wasn't in the class."

I glanced out the window. Missy had used the term "ruthless" to describe Hamburger's ambition, and that reputation had attached to him in the bar. Had Randy

Hamburger been ambitious and ruthless enough to deflect a cheating allegation by pinning it on his girlfriend?

"So, Doyle was cheating, but it was Hamburger who turned her in? Is that it?"

"Seems like it."

"That's a long way from Missy's story."

"It covers all of the facts as we know them."

"And what about Missy? She holds a mortal grudge against Hamburger because of what he did to her friend?"

DP stroked his jawline and mused for a moment.

"Doyle and Hamburger are taking Con Law and they're dating," he said. "That means they're studying together, doesn't it?

"Probably."

"Sounds to me like they were both cheating. Missy got wind of what they were up to and turned them both in."

"I don't think so. She says Doyle was her friend. She wouldn't turn on her friend."

DP paused.

"She's cute, isn't she? Missy, I mean."

"Yeah, she's cute. So what?"

"Don't let her play you, Joth."

"She's not gonna play me."

I responded too hastily, and DP saw it.

He nodded.

"Okay. Just sayin'."

I got up and began pacing across the well-worn rug.

"Okay, maybe Hamburger and Doyle were both cheating. And let's assume Doyle was pressured not to return to school or face expulsion. But what happened to Hamburger?"

"Nothing. Graduated number one in his class."

"So, the girlfriend got the boot and he skated?"

"Sure," he said. "He's the school's golden boy."

This made a certain amount of sense. No school wanted unfounded rumors following a student in good standing. And like any team, most law schools are going to protect their star. The school had too much invested in him.

"And then he did a federal clerkship?"

"No, he went straight into private practice."

"You'd think a guy first in his law school class would land a federal clerkship if he wanted one, which Missy says he did."

"Unless there was a red flag of some sort."

I let that sink in.

"Are you suggesting the school turned a blind eye to the cheating, but they got the word out to the federal judiciary that Hamburger wasn't to be trusted? That was his punishment?"

DP shook his head.

"Unless what happened at Tommy Kuhl's party was his punishment."

Chapter Eighteen

Halloween

I learned an unpleasant lesson early in my career. When a client arrives at your house unannounced and unexpected, he or she is telling you that they know where you live, which means they're delivering an implied threat.

Missy wasn't unhappy with me. At least I didn't think she was. She hadn't been a client long enough for that. But she came to my house because she wanted to deliver a message.

I had stocked up on Halloween candy and left the porch light on, but few trick or treaters came to my door. They rarely do. At 9:00, I turned off the outside light, made myself a drink, and put my feet up, watching the Caps with a bowl of mini candy bars on my lap.

The hockey game, a listless, low-scoring affair, hadn't captured my interest. I found myself thinking more about Missy than I wanted to or thought prudent. I tried to keep my focus on the factual and legal defenses available to her, but the story of Randy Hamburger branding his girlfriend a cheater many years ago continued to eat at me. This was not inconsistent with the man I had known. It reminded me of why the list of those not mourning his passing was so long.

I was trying to fit the pieces together when the doorbell rang. I switched on the overhead light, expecting to see a late arriving witch or skeleton, but it was Missy. I opened the door, and she stepped inside before I could assemble the words to invite her.

DP was right. Missy was a striking woman, whose physical attractions announced themselves anew each time I saw her. Her sullen mouth and the creases that fanned up between her eyebrows were etched by a lifetime of anger and suspicion, yet they added to her allure.

"Mind if I come in?"

She was already in the living room. I followed her in and turned off the TV.

"Drink?"

Her eyes followed mine to the cocktail glass on the side table beside my Barca Lounger.

"What are you having?"

"Dry Manhattan," I said.

It was a recipe I'd learned the last time I had a female visitor.

"Dry Manhattan!"

She crinkled her nose and laughed.

"A Dry Manhattan sounds about right."

My bar was set up on the island between the kitchen and the living room. I talked to her over my shoulder as I pulled together the ingredients.

"Do you know what's in a Dry Manhattan?"

"No, but I'll trust you. I have to, right? You're my lawyer."

I took my time with the drink shaker, wondering what had caused her change in attitude. I eyeballed the measures of rye and sweet vermouth, added a handful of ice, and gave it a half dozen vigorous shakes. I poured hers and refilled mine.

"Here's to justice," she said.

"Yes, indeed."

I took a long drink.

"How'd you know where I live?'

She took a swallow and winced.

"I'm a journalist. That's what I do."

"Don't con me, Missy. A journalist reports the facts. You're a purveyor of titillating opinions, and you love it."

She took another drink.

"Agreed."

"And you just happened to be passing by."

She reached into her purse and tossed a flash drive on the coffee table. The metal rimmed tag showed an early October date.

"Is that the radio show we were talking about?"

"Yup. The threat, if you still want to call it that, comes in just after the eighteen-minute mark."

I picked it up, walked across the room and locked it in a drawer in my desk.

"Exactly what did Randy Hamburger do to you to earn this lifetime of enmity?"

"I told you. He cheated in law school…"

"And he got away with it. So what?"

"I don't like cheaters."

"You've got bigger things than that to worry about."

"What does that mean?"

I shrugged. I wasn't sure what she wanted from me, and I wasn't about to chase it.

"It means somebody's been murdered and the police think the killer might be you. Sometimes, they get the wrong person, you know."

Her face fell, and she stared at me. Then she sat down in the armchair beside the TV.

"That wasn't what I wanted to hear."

"What did you want to hear?"

"I don't know. But I thought. You know…"

Her unfinished thought drifted away.

It took me a while to understand why I had reacted to her appearance with such hostility, but now I knew, and I had been right. Maybe Missy hadn't been a cheat, but she was manipulative, and I realized that was why she had come. I intended to head that off.

"Uh-huh. Tell me about Phyllis Doyle."

She paused, and her voice softened.

"What about her?"

"She was your roommate?"

"And my friend."

"So, you turned your friend and roommate in for cheating."

I expected this barb to provoke her, but it didn't.

"No, I turned in Randy. I told you that."

"Why?"

She took a drink.

"Because he was cheating!"

"Cheating on you, maybe."

She looked up sharply and her eyes flashed.

"He cheated on the Constitutional Law exam."

"You witnessed it?"

"Yes."

"Your story doesn't make sense, Missy. You weren't even in the class."

"He was cheating."

How'd you find out?"

"I don't remember."

I waited. I waited for almost a minute. I was ready to wait all night.

"Randy got a copy of the exam questions the night before."

"How did he do that?"

"I don't know."

"Yes, you do."

As she shifted her weight in the chair, I saw a parallel to the interview subjects she loved to put on the griddle on her radio show. I let her twist.

"I don't know how it worked at your law school, but at Mason, after the professors put together the exam questions, they delivered them to the registrar's office. The registrar was responsible for assembling the actual test. The professors picked up the printed exams in the morning and distributed them to the class. Randy got to somebody there."

"Who?"

"I don't know."

"I want to know what happened, Missy. That's the price of the drink."

A decisive look came over her face and her posture stiffened. Impatient, I pushed the attack.

"Your story is that you accused Randy Hamburger of cheating in a class you weren't even in. What I don't understand is why you'd make up that lie."

Her anger cooled as suddenly as it had flared.

"Because he was cheating! Because he tried to blame it on my friend!"

"You accuse someone of cheating, you'd better be able to prove it."

"That's right, and I had him dead. But he was slick, even then."

She put a knuckle to her lips and her eyes wandered toward the window. This was something I hadn't seen before or expected to see: Missy Brewer vulnerable. Or perhaps she was donning the mantle of vulnerability.

"How'd he slip out of it?"

"Woman scorned."

"I'm sorry?"

"They'd been dating for most of the spring. God knows why she was dating him, but Phyllis was young and dumb, I guess."

"What happened?"

"It was an awful experience, an awful night. Phyllis woke me up at about two in the morning. She was frantic. She told me what he was going to do."

"So, they both cheated?"

"No. She was straight as an arrow, a real Puritan. She didn't know what to do. But I had an exam the next day, too. I told her she needed to go to the professor and went back to sleep. She was gone when I got up in the morning. She was in love with him."

"So, you turned them both in?"

"No, I blew the whistle on Randy. I didn't know she'd agreed to go along with it."

"Then what?"

"He was one step ahead. They found the exam questions in her backpack. Randy claimed he didn't know anything about it."

"But he aced the test?"

"Sure, but he aced every test. For all I know, he was cheating on all of them."

"And Phyllis?"

"She aced the test, too. But she was a C student. That didn't help."

"And it was just about that time that you dropped out of school."

"I withdrew."

"Why'd you do that?"

"I told you. I had this opportunity in the media."

"How did that happen?

Instead of answering, she stood moved to the couch, patting the cushion beside her.

"Why don't you sit over here?"
And then the doorbell rang.

Chapter Nineteen

Trick or Treat

"Trick or treaters," I said.

It was almost ten o'clock and too late for trick-or-treaters in my neighborhood. I went to the door and switched on the outdoor light, expecting to see a lone, skulking teenager, trolling for unclaimed candy with a pillow case. But it was Heather. I immediately let her in. She looked hard at Missy.

"Looks like I came at a bad time."

"Looks like you did," said Missy.

"Well, too bad. I need to talk to you, Joth. Right now."

Missy stood up, perplexed, and Heather held the door open for her. Missy looked at me.

"Heather, this is my client."

"I thought I was your client?"

I turned to Missy and tried again.

"This person has information I need to help you."

Heather glared at Missy as I said this. Missy was a tough, strong-willed woman, but Heather had a way of bending people to her will.

"Call me tomorrow, will you, Joth?"

"Sure, Missy."

And she left.

As Heather stepped in, she wrinkled her nose.

"What's that? Are you burning incense?"

"Gardenia, if I had to guess."

She followed the scent toward the door Missy had walked through.

"What did she want?"

"I'm not exactly sure."

I closed the door and locked it. Then, I turned to Heather.

"Looks like you could use a drink?"

"What are you drinking?"

I held up my glass.

"Dry Manhattan."

"Jesus Christ, Joth!"

She went to the refrigerator and came out with a beer in a brown glass bottle. She screwed off the top and took a long drink. I poured my Dry Manhattan down the sink and got another beer out of the fridge. She took the spot on the couch that Missy had occupied, and I sat in the chair across from her.

She looked drawn and pale, with dark circles beneath her eyes.

"I think I might need a lawyer after all."

"What happened?"

"Do you remember Beth McGillis?"

I didn't, but taking the hint, I dredged my memory and called up a fuzzy recollection from when Heather and I were dating. I couldn't put a face or context to it.

"Name rings a bell. So what?"

She had something in her hand: a rectangular envelope about four by six inches. She flipped it at me, and I picked it up off the floor. It was addressed to Heather at her home. The address was written with a blue Sharpie in a bold confident hand. Inside was a card, professionally printed on heavy blue paper.

"GUESS WHO'S TURNING 40!?" it read.

Printed on the next line, in a slightly smaller font:

"Your presence is required at 1001 Balfour Circle for the Grand Reveal!"

This was followed by the date: next Saturday night.

A final line on the invitation read: "It's a surprise and time is of the essence!"

I wasn't sure what to make of it, or what Heather wanted from me.

"Sounds like fun. Are you going?"

"You know who lives at that address?"

"I'm guessing the answer is Beth McGillis."

She nodded and mused.

"Beth McGillis. I haven't heard from her in five years and now I'm invited me to her birthday party?"

"Hey, you're in demand."

"Take a look at the return address."

I turned the envelope over: 1001 Balfour Circle.

"Okay."

"You know where that is?"

"No idea."

"It's in the cul de sac on the other side of the woods from Tommy Kuhl's house."

Now I caught on. This was the address I popped out at after following the path through the woods from the scene of Hamburger's murder.

"Hmm," I said. "Some sort of joke? Or is she trying to retrieve the friendship?"

"How about none of the above? Do you know there's a path that goes through the woods from Kuhl's house to Beth's?"

"And?"

"Somebody's trying to set me up, Joth."

"Slow down. Who's trying to set you up?"

"If I knew that, I wouldn't be here."

She got up and paced the floor in front of the fireplace.

"It won't be long before some smart cop decides that the killer parked there and dragged Hamburger's dead body through the woods to Kuhl's backyard. Then, that cop's gonna tie it to me because I've been there before, and I know the neighborhood."

I got the sense that Heather was overreacting, and this was something she rarely did. I believed that the police were focused on another suspect: the woman who'd just left my house. I couldn't tell Heather that, but I wanted to turn down the temperature.

"Okay. I'll look into it."

"That's it? You'll look into it?"

"It's Halloween! What do you want me to do?"

She sighed.

"You're right."

I knew I owed her more than that.

"Is Sue making any progress on her investigation?"

"I don't know. She won't tell me anything."

"Is it possible that this is making you a little anxious?"

She thought for a moment, then laughed lightly.

"Well, if I'm going to act like a fool, I guess it's best that I do it in front of you."

"We've been through worse together."

"I suppose we have."

She sat down and shook her head.

"I just can't shake the idea that if I'm out of the way, Sue's the new CA. She's always wanted the top job."

"That's not going to happen."

"Not unless something happens to me. Like maybe I get accused of a felony."

"Come on. You think Sue's gonna use this to take you down?"

"She's capable of it."

"One thing about Sue. She's a pro."

"What you need to do is figure out who killed Hamburger," Heather said. "After that, everything will take care of itself."

This was the same thing I'd been telling myself for a week. I thought about the woman who'd just left my house. The argument against Missy would exonerate Heather, but the opposite was also true.

"What can you do to help me?"

"You've got to remember, Joth, I'm on the back bench. I'm not supposed to be involved in this."

"Good, you can leave it to me."

She looked toward the door. Missy's scent still hung in the air.

"Unless that's a mistake."

"Don't worry about Missy. She's just a source of information."

I figured that counted as a white lie, but feeling the need to lie to Heather was a red flag. If Heather didn't find something to keep her busy, she was going to drive us both crazy. With that in mind, I recalled my discussion with Frank Moran about the strychnine still held in the Luigi evidence file.

"I'd like to figure out where the strychnine came from. I was talking to Frank Moran, and he reminded me of a cold case, named Luigi."

The suggestion that it was not only unresolved but unresolvable grated on Heather.

"It's not a cold case. It's in process."

"Okay. Here's the point. Maybe there's some indication in the evidence file as to the source of the strychnine. The stuff that killed Hamburger might have come from the same place."

Her eyes brightened.

"Have you checked it out?"

"You know I can't get into the evidence room without supervision. But you can."

"Yeah, I can do that."

"Let me know what you find out."

She nodded.

"Just check the packaging, Heather. We need a place to start, and that might be it. If we identify the source, maybe we can find out who bought it."

"Okay. You know, I feel much better when there's a plan. Now, what about Beth's party? Do you think I should go?"

I thought about it. If this was some kind of set up, it was hard to see who was behind it or what they intended to achieve.

"If Hamburger was still alive, if none of this had happened, would you go?"

"I don't know. I haven't seen her in years. But I don't think this is a coincidence."

"Did you separate on bad terms?"

"Oh no, nothing like that. We just drifted apart."

I looked again at the envelope. Her presence was "required" and not requested, as was the usual formulation. The "Grand Reveal" was obviously bait, but for what?

"I don't see how you can pass. Maybe you'll learn something."

Heather got up, loitering for a minute, her car keys dangling from a lanyard in her hand.

"There's one more thing. Do you think you could go with me?"

"Go *with* you?"

"Or we could arrive separately. I just need some cover."

"Isn't that Peter's job?"

"Not lately."

I looked again at the invitation. The party was Saturday night. I had nothing else to do.

"That would be kind of awkward, wouldn't it? I haven't been invited."

"Oh, come on. When has that ever stopped you? I just need you to keep an eye on things, make sure I don't miss anything. Or screw up."

"I guess. I could meet you there."

"We can coordinate it, so we walk in at the same time, but not together."

"Okay. That works."

"Thanks, Joth."

I walked her toward the door. It took me a moment to turn the key in the lock and flip on the lights. When I turned around, I was face to face with her. Impulsively, she threw her arms around my neck and kissed me. She kissed me like she meant it. After a moment, I disentangled her arms from around my neck.

"I've been wanting to do that for a while."

"Give me warning next time, will you?"

I opened the door and held it for her. She paused. I could see her sifting through possible responses before she gave up and walked out into the night. As I shut the door, old feelings, long dead or suppressed, bubbled up again and I thought of what could have been, and what, perhaps, could still be.

I didn't hold that thought for long. Somehow, I was representing two people suspected of the same murder. It might be that the best defense for either of them was to point the finger at the other. The only way out of it was to find the real murderer, assuming it wasn't one of my clients.

Chapter Twenty

The Candy Man

The next morning, as I poured my first cup of coffee, I looked at the bright yellow plastic bowl of candy bars and gave silent thanks that my two unexpected visitors the night before had distracted me from gorging on them all. I knew that if I didn't get rid of them, they'd be gone before another night passed. Fortunately, I knew a guy who could enjoy them all, and without a whiff of guilt or remorse. I put the flash drive Missy had given me in my pocket, picked up the bowl, and headed to work.

I shared the first floor with a trusts and estates lawyer, named Mitch Tressler. Mitch was about my age, and like me, unmarried and unlikely to ever be married. His practice had been slow since I'd known him, and his slovenly personal habits and a gambling addiction didn't help. I found him behind his desk in his dark and cluttered office.

"Halloween's over, Mitch!"

I don't know why I thought that comment would break the spell. The blinds were pulled down and the only light came from a mis-matched pair of green shaded lamps on his credenza. His desk was crowded with so many stray objects it looked like a staging ground for still life paintings by Flemish masters. I noticed a plaster skull, an hourglass, and a guttered candle in a brass candlestick holder. Mitch was a man obsessed with death.

He looked up.

"What do you want?'"

"Nice to see you, too."

I moved some unopened law books and found a place on his desk for the candy bowl. He tilted his chin up to peer over the rim and thrust a hand in. He picked out a Three Musketeer and studied it with the air of a boy who'd found a cockleshell in a tide pool.

"What have we got here?"

"Unclaimed Halloween goodies. I thought you'd enjoy them."

His expression soured.

"Is that a comment on my weight?"

"No. I just don't eat the stuff."

"You should. It's good for you."

He peeled off the silver wrapper and popped the whole bar into his mouth.

"If you ate some candy once in a while you wouldn't be such a bitter pill to be around."

Mitch was one of the few people I knew who I'd let talk to me that way, but he usually didn't because he frequently needed my help.

"Mitch, you don't have enough friends to piss off one of the few you've got."

"I've got better friends than you."

This intrigued me. As far as I knew, he had no friends.

"I'm sure you do."

"A friend who sends me work."

I didn't send Mitch work because I couldn't trust him to handle it competently.

"Yeah, who's that?"

'Mike Purina."

"Mike Purina? Wilkins, Davis, and Purina?"

He popped another candy bar with the self-satisfied air of a house cat.

"That's right."

Wilkins, Davis, and Purina was a small, general practice firm in Springfield. There were some good lawyers in that firm, but Purina, a trust and estate lawyer with a reputation for cutting ethical corners, wasn't one of them.

"I thought Purina got suspended."

"He did. It doesn't mean people don't still call him."

"I see. So, he sends the work to you, knowing you won't steal the client?"

Purina was a crafty guy, which is why he got suspended. What I really meant was that he knew Mitch wouldn't be capable of retaining the client relationship once Purina served his suspension. When he got his license back, he'd have no trouble peeling the clients away from Mitch.

"Something like that. What of it?"

The Wilkins firm didn't have any other trusts and estates lawyers, but my curiosity had been piqued.

"I suppose he's keeping the good stuff in the firm?"

He was insulted by my tone, as I knew he would be.

"*Au contraire*. He sent me a trust for a non-dependent family member this morning."

"Oh yeah? For who?"

He folded his arms across his chest with a great show of embattled principle.

"A little bird gave it to me."

"A bird?"

"Let's say a wren. I can't tell you any more than that. It's privileged."

I failed to stifle a laugh and he turned red.

"You staying in the black with Jimmie Flambeau?"

This may have been a punch below the belt because I learned of Mitch's gambling problem through a professional connection, but legal niceties like ethical concerns seemed to fade when he was involved.

"As a matter of fact, I am."

"Is that right?"

"Jimmie gave me a tip on a prop bet, just yesterday."

Mitch didn't realize that Jimmie regularly offered small sure things to help his clients break losing streaks and keep the thrill alive. That hook hadn't set in my mouth. I turned away, uninterested.

"It has to do with your girlfriend."

That stopped me.

"She's not my girlfriend. Anyway, she's gonna win. Her opponent's dead."

"That's not the bet."

"What is it then?"

"He's only offering it to preferred clients."

There was not much I could do to help a guy who courted disaster without even recognizing the danger.

"Okay Mitch. Enjoy the candy."

I walked away gritting my teeth. Jimmie never intentionally pushed my buttons, but he was blind to my no go zone. Profiting off Heather's misfortune—if that's what he was doing—would provoke a confrontation I might later regret. I decided to put it out of my mind, but deciding and doing it were two very different things.

Chapter Twenty-One

Secrets in the Attic

DP Tran liked to do things the old-fashioned way, and since the November rent was now due, I climbed the dim, narrow stairs to the second floor. He was behind his desk at the near end of the room, working out a problem on a legal pad. The sun streamed in through the windows in the same wall that Mitch kept shuttered on the floor below.

He put his pen down, folded his hands behind his head, and kicked his feet up on his desk. He had a hopeful look on his round, sallow face. My appearance in his office usually signaled a problem to solve, and he liked nothing better, except to have the rent paid on time.

I slid my check into the middle of his desk. He looked at it briefly, nodded, and put it in his top desk drawer.

"You know who else paid today?"

It was an easy question. DP only had one other tenant.

"On time! Is that a first?"

"Pretty nearly."

Friend in the Bullseye

"Business is booming, I guess."

"Yeah, Mike Purina sent him a case and promised him a lot more."

"Mitch told me he's doing a complex trust."

"And for a friend of yours, too."

I took a seat across from him.

"Yeah? Who's that?"

"Tommy Kuhl."

"Tommy Kuhl's no friend of mine."

"I saw you at his party."

"You were there?"

"I was Zorro."

I remembered a black-masked acrobat slashing Zs indiscriminately with a rapier.

"I didn't know you knew him."

"I don't. And he doesn't like Asians."

He smiled and bobbed the hairless ridges above his eyes.

"I wouldn't have gone if he'd invited me," he said.

"Then, you saw what happened with Hamburger?"

"Only from a distance. Tell you the truth, I was enjoying Kuhl's liquor and not paying much attention."

I chuckled. DP so rarely missed a trick that he sometimes seemed inhuman.

"I guess that was the plan, that everyone would be having too much fun to notice a murder right in front of their eyes."

"It's a plan that seemed to work."

"So far," I said.

"Everybody was there. Did you see Sue?"

"Sue who?"

"Sue Crandall. She was Little Red Riding Hood."

I remembered the woman in the scarlet hood and cape dancing with Jimmie Flambeau dressed as a red devil. So, the lamb was being courted by the wolf. Or were they both wolves?

"That's interesting information."

"Not only that…"

"I know. She was dancing with Flambeau. I think it might be time I paid Jimmie a visit."

"You still represent him?"

"You think he's a suspect?"

"Flambeau's always a suspect."

That was all I needed: another client suspected of the same murder. But he was also a source of information not available elsewhere that might lead me to the killer.

"I'm always careful."

"Yeah. Has he still got that stolen painting hanging in his office?"

He was referring to the Manet I'd once seen hanging above his safe. With my assistance, DP had tried to recover it. It was the kind of caper that could make a PI's career, but we had been a day late. He hadn't forgotten that near miss and he never would.

"Not the last time I was there."

"I thought he might try to claim the reward. If he did, he'd use you as the intermediary."

A bronze eagle from a Napoleonic battle standard, stolen in the same 1990 Boston art heist, was sitting in the bookshelf in my office and whenever DP reminded me of this, I got nervous.

"Probably."

"Probably? Certainly. Let me know if it reappears."

As I got up to go, DP resumed his work, but he had a final comment.

"By the way, I found Phyllis Doyle."

I sat down again.

"Missy's law school roommate? You know where she lives?"

"Sure do."

That was a shocker. So was the next thing he said.

"She changed her name. Goes by Beth McGillis now."

I'd heard that name just the night before. Beth McGillis was the long lost-friend who had unexpectedly invited Heather to her 40th birthday party.

Chapter Twenty-Two

The Tale of the Tape

DP waited as I processed this information, then started again.

"She got married. I'm guessing that with a new last name, she started using a different first name as a way of getting a fresh start after what happened in law school. That's all I've got right now."

That was a lot. I didn't speak and DP let the silence linger, reading the response on my face.

"Looks like you know her."

"I know who she is. She's a friend of Heather's. Or was."

DP got up and walked to the window. He stood with his hands on his hips, looking down on busy Wilson Boulevard.

"You know where she lives?"

"Sure do."

He spun around to look at me.

"This doesn't sound like a coincidence."

"That's what Heather said when I saw her last night. She got invited to her birthday party, but she hasn't seen her in years."

"What does she think?"

"She thinks somebody is trying to set her up for Hamburger's murder."

It was difficult for me to believe that anyone thought Heather had murdered her opponent or that she was in any real legal jeopardy, but DP lacked my bias and had a different perspective.

"Maybe she's right. Does she know who?"

"A woman in her position makes a lot of enemies."

"Yes, she does."

I shoved my hands in my pockets, where my fingers felt the flash drive Missy had given me the night before. I'd almost forgotten about it. I pulled it out and held it up.

"Here's something else on our task list."

"Is that what I think it is?"

I nodded.

"Missy dropped it off last night."

I tossed it to him. He held it up to the light and examined it like a rare jewel. DP had extensive electronic equipment set up behind his desk. As I closed the door, he plugged the flash drive into the player, started it, and adjusted the volume.

"It's at the eighteen-minute mark."

"Don't you think we should listen to the whole thing?"

For a moment, I attributed this to prurient interest, but then I realized that DP was only being thorough. He never let himself get too close to the players. His precision served as a quick wake-up call for me.

The recording, which excluded commercial breaks on the live broadcast, ran about 40 minutes. It was as tough to take and as compelling as the Zapruder film of JFK's assassination. Missy began with her assessment of a DC political issue, expounding her views with the kind of rage that endeared her to her followers. She knew the truth and those who denied it were fools. There was no effort at reason or persuasion, only the force of her personality and the intensity of her conviction. Her first and second guests were people on the fringe of the DC political scene, who appeared to be serving as a chorus to punctuate her dramatic screeds.

As the 18-minute mark approached, Missy and a former DC Council candidate were discussing the Supreme Court and the problems associated with the lifetime tenure of federal judges. Missy's collaborator commented that they were "all for sale."

"Not all," Missy said, "and not all the time, but when you can figure out where their interest lies, you can predict their vote."

"At least from what you've heard."

Missy's voice rose.

"They're all in it to line their own pockets. Start with that. It's just an instinct with them."

"Something they're born with?"

"That's it. When I was in school, I knew one of the all-time skunks. He's running for Commonwealth Attorney in Arlington, but he'd probably be a federal judge already if it wasn't for me."

The guest picked up the cue.

"What happened?"

"He was a cheat. He was a cheat from the start. That's all I'm going to say about him. He ruined the life of a young law student along the way with no more remorse than if you trapped a mouse in your kitchen. He's not fit for the office he's running for. He's not fit to be alive."

Missy's producer used this peroration to segue to a commercial break. When it ended, Missy and her guest had moved on to something else.

DP turned the player off and removed the flash drive.

"That woman's carrying some anger."

"How about the person she's talking about? That's got to be the woman who is now calling herself Beth McGillis."

I paused and changed topics.

"Heather wants me to go with her to the party Saturday night."

DP whistled.

"That sounds dangerous. For at least a couple of reasons."

"You're right. But I don't like the way the tide is running. Sue and her team are working hard at something."

"Yeah. You think she's focused on Heather?"

"She wants Heather's job. Heather's right about that. But if Sue clears this case, she'll have the credentials to run against Heather in the next election. Missy's the obvious target. I can't wait around while Sue ties the noose."

"What's the next step?"

"McGillis' party. Maybe you should crash it and help keep an eye on things."

"Last time I crashed a party, someone was murdered."

"And maybe by crashing another one, we can solve it."

DP wasn't convinced.

"Let me make some calls first."
That's what I was hoping he'd say.

Chapter Twenty-Three

Odds Are

When I got back to my office, the flashing light on the console of my desk phone told me I'd missed a call. I checked the number: Jimmie Flambeau. I sometimes believed that his ears burned when I talked about him.

Jimmie didn't leave messages. He didn't have to. He knew that his phone number alone would serve as a summons. He used me as a source of inside information in the same way I used DP. That was part of the reason he put me on retainer, but it was a symbiotic relationship. I was usually seeking something from him, too, and he was generally willing to oblige, so long as his interests weren't compromised.

I went outside and took the short walk up Wilson Boulevard, where Hamburger's maroon and black campaign signs still dotted the median. Faded and tattered, they looked like the marks left by a fatal disease. Immediately after Hamburger's death, Heather had quietly ordered her signs removed.

The last time I visited Jimmie, I found myself on surprisingly good terms with his usually inscrutable assistant, Helen. I didn't expect my luck to continue, but it did. She gave me the cheerful smile of a co-conspirator, which made me wonder if Jimmie's intensity and constant suspicion were starting to outweigh what I assumed was compensation worthy of a princess.

"When I was here last week, Jimmie was having trouble with the troops."

Helen's green lacquered fingernails flew along the keyboard.

"It's not gotten any better, and his mood hasn't exactly improved either."

I thought about the prop bet he was offering on Heather and decided to let it drop. Being Jimmie Flambeau was sometimes its own punishment.

"Well, I'll see what I can do to help."

She shot me a quick smile.

"Somebody's in there, but he never stays long."

Before I could come up with a glib response, Ish McGriff, looking spiffy and trim in his khaki pants and a dark brown sheriff's deputy shirt, emerged from the back office. He stopped and scowled when he saw me, but then summoned a congenial expression.

"Hello, Proctor."

"Ish. How are things?"

"Fine."

He gestured toward Jimmie's office.

"Just serving some papers."

As a sheriff's deputy, Ish had the perfect cover to moonlight for a guy who often received official documents courtesy of the sheriff's office.

"Sure."

He looked at Helen like she was the main course at the Saturday night buffet at Golden Corral, which I could see unnerved her. No wonder she treated all of Jimmie's visitors with the same thinly veiled contempt. She buzzed Ish out and buzzed me in without another word to either of us.

Jimmie didn't look up. He had his chin on his fist, studying his computer screen. I sat down in my usual chair and noted that out-of-date calendar still occupying the place where the Manet once hung. With an impulsive gesture, he slammed the laptop shut, leaned back in his chair, and glared at me.

"I'm going to take a beating next Tuesday."

Next Tuesday was Election Day.

"What's the problem? Heather can't lose."

"That's the problem."

"I thought you supported her?"

"Sure, but I didn't think she'd win."

"Is that what they call hedging your bets?"

He smiled as if I'd complemented him.

"Something like that. So, the question is, counsellor: do I have to pay?"

I looked at him curiously, wondering when the real question would come.

"Gambling contracts are unenforceable in Virginia. You know that."

"But if I stiff my clients…"

He nodded gravely. As I waited for more, I realized he was looking to me for business advice, not legal advice. I wasn't sure if that made me feel more or less uncomfortable.

"That's not good in any business," I said.

"I'm thinking about offering my clients the chance to double down on some sort of follow-up bet that seems more favorable to them."

Recalling Mitch's comment on the prop bet, I guessed that Jimmie wanted my opinion on something he had already decided to do.

"Such as what?"

He eyed me for a long moment.

"Like, maybe how long Burke keeps the job?"

So, this was the prop bet he'd offered Mitch.

"It's a four-year term, Jimmie. She's not going anywhere."

"You feel confident about that?"

"Unless you know something I don't."

Of course, Jimmie always knew things no one else did. That was how he made his living. He looked away and shifted some paper to his out box.

"A lot of things could happen."

"Such as?"

"Look, I'm going to get killed on the straight-up election bet. She's gonna win. I had it figured the other way. Now, I'm giving short odds that she won't stay in the job. People like the idea of a big pay-off on a small wager, even if it's unlikely they'll win. They like the action, Joth. The juice is the thing. And what the hell, a lot of things could happen. She could become a judge, be hired by a big firm, or take a job with the federal government. She could decide to spend more time with her kids. Or work on her marriage."

I remembered what Heather had said about opening Proctor & Burke, or Burke & Proctor. Either would be okay with me. Jimmie waited until he caught my eye.

"Or go into private practice."

I didn't mind doing Jimmie's legal work, but I'd be damned if I'd let him use me as source of odds about a friend's career. Especially Heather's. So, I took a shot.

"What did Kelleher tell you about Heather?"

"Christine? Christine's a smart lady."

"Meaning she knows what's good for her?"

"I hope so."

He rocked in his chair, holding my eyes. We were playing poker now, his favorite game, and the stakes were information.

"You and Sue looked pretty cozy at Kuhl's party."

"She didn't know who she was dancing with."

"But you did."

"Of course."

"I thought she was your sworn enemy."

"Why do you think I danced with her?"

"Maybe you should take bets on how long she'll last."

He sat up. Now, I was talking his language.

"Or which one will last longer."

Or was this the bet he'd offered Mitch?

"Commonwealth Attorney's serve a long time around here," I said. "Deputies are a dime a dozen."

"She's got a big case on her hands right now."

"Crandall? Yes, she does."

"You think she's up to the challenge?"

"You were the one dancing with her."

"She didn't tell me shit. And believe me, I pushed for any hint I could get."

I thought about it and tossed my head. Jimmie was getting information from someone. Kelleher had thrown her lot in with Crandall. Jimmie knew that, and he knew better than to trust her. If it wasn't Kelleher, it had to be

Ish. I recalled that Ish had told me how dangerous she was. Dangerous to whom? I wondered.

"You better be careful. Crandall pulled Kelleher's career out of the dumpster. Christine's likely to feel loyal to her."

Jimmie swiveled toward the window and stared out at the autumn landscape.

"I'm not worried about that."

"What did Ish tell you?

"The problem with Ish is, he's a sheriff's deputy. He doesn't know that much."

"Did he tell you it was Sue who got Christine out of the evidence room and back on the street?"

This was what Betty had told me. Jimmie didn't seem surprised.

"I keep my ear to the ground."

"I'd be careful about counting on her loyalty."

"She can't turn on me. I've got too much on her."

"She's gonna have to prove to Sue that she made the right decision to bring her onto her team."

"Crandall's not the CA. She has one case, and it's got nothing to do with me. Okay, so I have to be careful with Christine. I know that. She's a cop. Besides, I'm always careful. Especially with you."

He gave me a hard glance, then shifted his weight in the chair.

I figured he was right. Kelleher could shape her future, but she couldn't run from her past. It was a question of knowing who her friends were. If she miscalculated, she had as much to lose as Jimmie.

I glanced toward the calendar on the wall over the safe.

"What happened to the Manet?"

He shifted his eyes away from me.

"Oh that. I'm working to return it."

"Return it?"

"To the museum."

Return it?

That didn't seem to require much work. He could just call the museum and claim the reward.

"You want my help with that?"

"Maybe. Let me think about it."

It might make sense for a guy like Jimmie to have an intermediary in the negotiation. But that assumed he still had the painting and intended to return it. He wouldn't do that without first lining up a massive reward. Or if he needed a get out of jail free card.

I got up, feeling a little disgusted with myself. Jimmie could be a genial and entertaining guy, and he was such a great source of information that I sometimes forgot just how unprincipled he was. I was about to tell him exactly that when I noticed something on the edge of his desk. It was face down, but based on the size, shape, and color of the envelope, it looked identical to the invitation Heather had received.

"What's that?"

Jimmie scooped it up and swept it into his top desk drawer. His face set in a pugnacious expression.

"None of your damn business."

I felt like I needed a shower.

Chapter Twenty-Four

Shirlington

While sitting in my office, musing on the state of affairs, I couldn't shake the recognition that I had what the academics like to call an ethical dilemma. I represented two people who could reasonably be suspected of committing the same murder, and it was safe to assume that the picture would only get brighter for one of them when it got darker for the other.

Only a fool or an incompetent would allow himself to get into such an obvious and unsustainable conflict, but facts can be annoying things. Had Missy Brewer finally avenged herself on her old roommate's boyfriend, a man she claimed she hardly knew and a woman she'd lost track of? What else explained her kaleidoscopic pattern of ever-changing lies?

If so, it would make life much easier for Heather, but if Missy got wind of my double dealing on Heather's behalf, she could put my livelihood in jeopardy with a single phone call. She wouldn't hesitate if she thought it would get her off the griddle.

I was in too deep to withdraw from either representation, and my often-faulty instinct for self-preservation told me that the only way out was to find the real killer and do it quickly.

I wanted to talk to Heather. I always wanted to talk to Heather, even when I had nothing to say. I called her the next morning.

"I'm gonna do it today."

Her voice sounded tight and irritated.

"Do what?"

"Check the evidence room. Isn't that why you called?"

"I wanted to know if I can buy you a drink."

She hesitated. Remembering how she had left my house on Halloween night, I scrambled to avoid a misunderstanding.

"This is purely business, Heather."

"But that can change, right?"

"Heather, you don't need to add another problem to your list."

"I suppose not. Today?"

I heard her chair creak as she leaned forward to consult her calendar.

"I can do that. Something up?"

"Just want to check in on a few things."

She knew that meant yes. There was no fooling Heather.

"You know the Shirlington Grande?"

"Of course."

"Meet you there in an hour?"

"See you then."

Shirlington was a contemporary, mixed-use community that butted up against Interstate 395 in the southern part of the county. Built around Campbell Avenue, a walkable, bikeable central street, Shirlington is home to dozens of shops and restaurants, the grandest of which is the Shirlington Grande, where the rectangular mahogany bar was the centerpiece of the first floor.

It was early by Shirlington Grande standards, and the usual crowd of swingers and would-be adulterers had yet to assemble. I took a vacant stool.

Darla was planted right in the middle of it like a lynx at the zoo. I recognized her as she approached, but what was worse, she recognized me. Six months earlier, I'd met a target there for lunch. I'd used an alias, and to my amazement, she remembered it.

"Hi. I haven't seen you in a while."

"Darla, isn't it?"

"That's right."

"You got my name wrong. It's Joth Proctor."

The bar at the Grande had a reputation as a pick-up spot, popular with the gay and straight communities.

Darla shook her head vigorously and smiled.

"No. I make my living remembering names and faces. But if that's your story, it's okay with me."

"Bourbon straight, please."

She mixed it and delivered my drink with a wry smile and a wink.

***

As usual, Heather was punctual, but I was early enough that I'd polished off my first drink before she got there. As she sat on the vacant stool beside me, I noticed rings under her eyes that spoke of sleeplessness. She had attempted to compensate with a trip to her hair stylist. The elaborate wave that swept away from her elegant cheekbones enhanced the strawberry highlights she'd added since Halloween.

She took note of the empty cocktail glass in front of me.

"I hope that was your first."

"What are you drinking?"

She thought about it, which surprised me. Not only was she usually decisive about alcohol, but she rarely drank during working hours.

Darla approached with my second.

"I'll have what he's having."

Heather had taken some time with her clothing, too. Inevitably stylish but never flashy, she favored pants suits, like the one she wore today. Red was reserved for important court matters. Today, she was wearing forest green, a color that showed off her complexion and strawberry hair. It was an alluring combination, and I needed to put it out of my mind.

She helped with her first question.

"Didn't you get into a fight here once?"

"It wasn't really a fight."

"One punch doesn't make a fight?"

"He swung at me first."

"That's not how I remember it. I had to do some fast talking to get you out of that one."

This wasn't quite true, but I'd forgotten that brief dust-up with a drunken Capitals fan. Anyway, I was here to pull her fat out of the fire, not to revisit our past.

"So, I owe you one?"

"I think we're about even, but I'm not keeping score."

"Is Crandall still keeping you in the dark on the Hamburger murder?"

"Yup. Betty, too. But Betty thinks Sue's getting close to an arrest."

That was news. I wondered if she'd dug up as much on Missy Brewer as I had. Knowing Sue, that would probably be enough.

"What's Kelleher's role in all this?"

"She and Sue are friends. At least I think they are." Heather shrugged.

"Sue's entitled to put her own team together."

"How come you pulled her off the street?"

"Because she was taking money from Jimmie Flambeau. But I'm sure you're aware of that."

"Why didn't you fire her?"

"I re-assigned her. Better to have her inside the tent pissing out, as somebody once said."

"LBJ, I think."

"Well, she doesn't need to make me happy anymore."

"She will when this case is over and Sue's back to being just another assistant."

"Unless she thinks that day will never come."

"Is this case going to make that much noise?"

"It already has. Don't you read the papers? It's as if this is the only case my office is handling."

She sighed, then continued.

"You know, I've had this job for a long time. Sometimes, people just want a new face and a new voice. Sue probably thinks that if she gets a conviction, she'll be set up to take me on in the next election. She's probably right."

That would be especially true if she pinned the murder on a rabble-rousing misanthrope who'd spent the last several years dousing the internet with a different kind of poison. Missy was a made-to-order defendant, and Sue might not care whether she had committed the crime or not.

The drinks came. Heather raised hers in a toast, then put it back down. She wanted to be sociable, but without violating her usual practice.

"I've got some other news to deliver."

"Okay, let's hear it."

"I went down to the evidence room and took a look in Luigi."

"And?"

"And the strychnine's gone."

"Gone?"

"Gone. It was kept in a sealed glass vial. I found the vial but it's empty."

"Somebody took the contents?"

"More likely someone switched vials."

"Any idea how long ago?"

"No. No one's signed into that file for a month."

I thought about it.

"Who was the last one to sign in?"

"Frank Moran."

"Moran?"

"Surprised?"

I was, but I wasn't sure why. He was the investigating officer.

"You know Frank's retired, right?"

"Yeah, just about the time he was in the evidence room."

"Do you know why?"

I waited for whatever else was coming.

"Evidence tampering. He'd been dipping into the evidence closet for years, skimming off cocaine for personal use."

"I hadn't heard that."

"It's the sort of thing we prefer to keep quiet and try to forget."

We both thought for a moment.

"Are you suggesting that Moran accessed the Luigi strychnine and used it to kill Hamburger?"

She shook her head.

"I'm only noting that Moran's a guy who can take that kind of risk. I assume Sue is tracking down his relationship with the late, lamented Mr. Hamburger."

Heather's information begged a question.

"Once someone's in the evidence room, can they get into another case without signing into that file?"

"It's not supposed to happen that way. That's why we have an officer on the desk. But it happens. I'm aware of it."

"Wait a minute. That's where you put Kelleher, right? On the evidence desk."

She saw my point and sat up.

"So, she had…"

Heather finished the point for me.

"Unrestricted access. She was the only one who could access evidence without signing in."

"Can you get a list of everyone who's signed into the evidence room in the past two months?"

"Way ahead of you, Joth."

She passed me a manilla file containing a stapled sheaf of computer-generated pages. It was a list of names and dates.

"This is the list, but I'm not sure it helps. It includes dozens of cops and detectives, every prosecutor, and who knows how many defense attorneys."

I glanced through it. The names of many of the lawyers I knew were on the list, including mine. Heather was on it, too, multiple times.

"You think the killer used the poison from Luigi?"

"If so, it's a black eye for me. It's my job to keep that stuff secure."

That was true. I wondered if the list eliminated Missy as a suspect.

"Doesn't that mean the killer is someone in the legal community?"

After staring at her glass for several seconds, Heather lifted it and took a healthy drink.

"Or someone with access to a person in the legal community."

By the way she pursed her lips and furrowed her brow, I could see that she was already considering that possibility. Missy didn't have that kind of access. How could she have gotten it?

"We can talk about where we are on Saturday night. You're still taking me to that party, right?"

"Wouldn't miss it."

I asked about her kids, and we concluded with even smaller small talk. As I watched her go, I admired her stately, confidant posture. Then, I finished my drink and settled the tab.

"No luck today, huh?"

I looked up at Darla.

"Depends on what you mean by luck."

I stuck a rolled up $20 in an empty cocktail glass.

"I'll be back in about 20 minutes. Keep these two stools free, will you?"

Chapter Twenty-Five

Second Game of the Doubleheader

The Shirlington Grande was known for unique entrées, imaginative drinks and a wild singles scene, but I picked it because Missy's show was broadcast from a studio just down the street. I had a few choice things I wanted to say to her. Her show ran from 10:00 to 2:00.

By quarter of two, I had found Missy's car in an underground, secure lot, angled across white lines marking two parking spaces in the back corner. A woman espousing the opinions Missy did would be well advised to remain on guard, but whether she was fueled by ego or insecurity, she was the type to always opt for expedience over caution.

While I waited, I called DP.

"Heather told me the strychnine is gone from the Luigi evidence file."

DP swore.

"How is that possible?"

He was thinking out loud. A few seconds later, he spoke again.

"Does she know who the last person was to sign in?"

"Yeah. Frank Moran."

"Huh. That's something to think about."

"Because he took early retirement over an allegation that he tampered with evidence? You know anything about that?"

I heard him typing into his computer.

"It was a cocaine case. Moran botched the chain of custody and that's how they learned he was dipping into the evidence. The guy walked."

"It happens."

"Captain Reynolds lost his mind. He moved Frank to vice until he could learn to handle evidence properly."

"That sounds kind of petty."

"We're talking about Dick Reynolds. Anyway, Frank and Reynolds have been butting heads for years. Frank finally had enough, and he took early retirement."

"Why are you telling me this?"

"You know who the defense counsel was in the cocaine case?"

I didn't have a clue.

"Randy Hamburger."

"Frank had a beef with Hamburger?"

"Yeah, but so did a lot of people, including Captain Reynolds. Now, I've got something to tell you."

"It'll have to wait."

When Missy walked out of the studio at 2:10, I was leaning insouciantly against her silver Jag. I heard her approach before she came into view. Her short, tight skirt made her scurry and her short steps and high heels made a choppy noise on the concrete garage floor. When she looked up and saw me, she put a hand to her throat.

"Jesus Christ, you scared me."

"You got anything in particular to be scared about?"

"Just the state of my soul."

As she unlocked the car with her fob, I leaned against the driver's door. She directed me out of the way with a gesture of her open hand, but I didn't move.

"You got time for a drink?"

"I don't do well with unplanned meetings."

She sounded exasperated but wouldn't give me the satisfaction of showing surprise.

"I like to address surprising information promptly and directly."

"What information?"

"You know somebody named Beth McGillis?"

She stared at me, but I didn't flinch. To her credit, neither did she. I sensed she was already moving on to the next dodge.

"What about her?"

"They've abolished the death penalty in Virginia, Missy, but juries love to put murderers in prison for life."

She digested that and looked at her watch.

"I can spare you half an hour and two drinks."

"That should be enough."

We went across the street to the Shirlington, each waiting for the other to speak. The bar was filling up with unattached men and women, but Darla had held the two stools.

"I'm drinking bourbon," I said. "It seems like a bourbon sort of day."

Missy nodded.

"That sounds about right."

I ordered, then turned to take a good look at her. She smiled, giving the impression of a person at ease.

"You like the high wire, don't you?"

"Yes. And I like working without a net."

"Yeah. But keep in mind that at that altitude, your first mistake can be your last."

Her face flashed the sullen expression of a teen caught skipping school.

"You think you're going to brazen this out, don't you?"

"I always have."

The drinks came.

"Maybe you don't need a lawyer."

"Maybe I don't."

I shook my head and sipped my drink.

"That makes it easy for me."

I got up and reached for my wallet.

"I'll send you back your retainer."

She put her hand on mine.

"Don't."

She took a long drink, then raised her finger for Darla and ordered another.

"Alright. I know I have a problem."

"You need to start acting like it."

"Maybe the cure is worse than the disease."

Missy took a deep breath. She was frightened, but she kept her fear below the surface.

"My stock in trade is my arrogance, my confidence, and my unwillingness to compromise. Right? I channel the frustrations of my listeners, and if I'm harassed by a corrupt government, it's because I'm fighting for the people. I only lose when my base of support abandons me, and that won't happen as long as I keep fighting."

"It sounds like you're looking forward to being indicted."

"Far from it. The more buzz I generate, the more my producer likes it, but he doesn't have to deal with the stress."

"So, all I have to do is make sure you don't go to jail."

She swallowed audibly.

"How can I go to jail? I didn't do anything."

"But you keep making it harder for me. Missy, I don't mind it when someone facing a felony charge fudges the facts around the edges, because I don't have to do the time if they're wrong. You don't know me, and there's too much at stake for you to not hedge your bets."

She swallowed again.

"You want to keep your options open. I get it. But once you start telling the big lies, then I can't tell where the truth begins and where it ends."

"Okay."

"But you just can't help it, can you? You can't stand it if anything or anybody gets an edge on you. Missy, the problem is, I can't seem to get it through your head that this is more than a PR problem."

"I know that."

"Is anything going to change?"

"I don't want to lose my job."

I was about to say that this should be the least of her concerns, but in that moment, it occurred to me that she might be willing to go to jail if she knew she could continue to host her radio show from her jail cell.

"You stand to lose a lot more than your job. Do you understand that?"

"I didn't kill him. I haven't given him two thoughts since I left school."

I studied her. Was this the face of a killer? She'd tried to summon her most school-girlish expression, but I looked past that, past the hard miles and the sadness and anger and disappointment that paved those miles. Selfish? That was self-evident. Spoiled and entitled? Certainly. But a murderer? There was a lot of anger in Missy, but hers were petty motives, and the remedies she sought to impose on those who offended her were equally childish. And that was why I didn't see her as a murderer. Revenge for her was sweetest when it was petty. Hamburger alive was a target for her wrath. Hamburger dead was as much a part of the past as eighth grade.

"A lot of innocent people get convicted of murder, Missy. Please don't make my job any harder than it has to be."

"Alright."

She appeared to have backed herself into a corner where she was willing to answer my questions honestly, but as tersely as possible. I could work with that.

"So, you found the job in radio after you left school?"

"That's right. I would never have been as successful in the law as I've been in the radio business. I just need to accept that."

I thought for a minute and finished my drink.

"There are three things you can do about your past, Missy: lie about it, including lying about it to yourself; confront it and deal with it; or ignore it. I don't think you're likely to confront it, and you need to stop lying about it because some people will draw the wrong conclusion. So, just don't talk about it. To anybody. Think you can handle that?"

"I have to admit that things are getting a little hot. Some people are asking about it."

She smiled when she said this, as if the roiling chaos was a badge of her success.

"Who?"

"My producer. People with the press."

"I know you've developed the ability to tell people to take a hike. Can you do that from now on? At least until this is over?"

"How long will that be?"

I assumed Sue wanted to bring an indictment before election day.

"I don't know. Crandall wants to make the biggest splash she can. Could be any day."

For someone with such an insatiable desire for attention, a week probably sounded like an eternity.

"Don't you have any contacts over there other than Burke?"

I thought about it; I thought about Christine Kelleher.

"I might. I'll do what I can. You need to lay low. Is that possible for you?"

"I'll try."

I started to get up.

"I've gotta go."

"Another date?"

"I'm afraid not."

"Thanks for the drink. And the advice."

"Are you going to take it? The advice, I mean?"

"I'm going to try to. How's that?"

She shook my hand with the stiff formality of a job candidate and a mask of imperturbability settled again over her face. It was an admirable display of self-control, but she looked totally drained.

I watched her leave. When she was gone, Darla strolled over.

"Another drink?"

"I don't think so, thanks."

She made herself busy mopping up an imaginary spill on the bar, then peeked up at me with a mischievous smile.

"Struck out twice today, huh? I doubt that happens very often."

"How much attention were you paying?"

"Not much. I just watch. I don't listen."

"And what did you think?"

"You seemed more interested in the second woman, but I think the first was better suited to you."

"Yeah? Why do you say that?"

"Chemistry, I guess. The woman with the strawberry hair? She likes you. The other one? I'm not so sure."

"Well, you're a little off base. They're both professional acquaintances."

She chuckled.

"Okay, if that's your story."

"What do you mean, you're not so sure about the second?"

"I don't know. Body language. Lack of eye contact."

"Don't trust her?"

She scratched her chin.

"I don't know if that's fair. I mean, I don't know her. For one night, that wouldn't matter."

My recent experiences with women were hardly conventional, but because Darla operated in the dark world of pick-ups and one-night stands, her insights were valuable.

I put out another probe.

"That young lady has a legal problem and I'm trying to help her."

Darla chuckled again, anticipating something sordid.

"Criminal?"

"How'd you guess?"

"Does she look like a guilty person to you?"

She ignored the question and instead reached under the bar, bringing out a Magic Eight Ball. She shook it, and as she did, she asked a question.

"Is this woman someone you can trust?"

It was the right question. She inverted the Eightball and read the message in the liquid filled window in the bottom of the globe.

" 'Outlook not so good.' "

"That's kind of what I figured."

Chapter Twenty-Six

Puck and Crisp

The next morning, I found Puck and Crisp seated on the couch in the reception area across from Marie's desk. Puck's pretty face wore an expression of prim dignity while Crisp looked ready to drink hot blood.

A joke heard occasionally among lawyers at law firms with a criminal and business practice is that reception areas should have a "sick" and a "well" side, as in a doctor's office, to keep the criminal defendants from infecting the others. This joke offends most criminal lawyers, as it does me, but I was secretly glad there was no one else in the reception area.

The two young women seemed to have dressed for shock effect. Long, lanky Crisp wore all black: tights, short skirt and a black wrap that was closer to a cape than a jacket. Her make-up was heavy and similarly grim, and she looked at me with undisguised contempt. Puck was in her familiar diaphanous snow white, but without the usual spangles or sparkles. She appeared cheerful and almost glad to see me.

Before I could finish a brief greeting, Crisp was on her feet.

"We need to see you privately."

That was certainly my preference.

"Come right in."

I held the door open, closed it behind them, and Puck took one of the client chairs without being told. Crisp stood with her hands on her hips, glaring at me as if she wanted to provoke a conflict.

I sat down behind my desk.

"What can I do for you two?"

Crisp leveled a long index finger at me.

"You have Puck's money?"

I glanced at the younger girl.

"Puck's money?"

"Her paycheck," said Crisp. "Her last paycheck. You took it from Dan."

I remembered and nodded.

"Yes, I have it. Dan gave it to me."

I unlocked my top desk drawer and removed it, still in the sealed payroll envelope.

"You were supposed to deliver it to her."

I recalled the afternoon when I tried to do so and addressed my answer to Puck.

"Yes, and I dropped by. Mr. Kuhl wanted me to give it to him, but I didn't feel comfortable doing that."

Crisp and Puck exchanged glances.

"Why not?"

Crisp asked the question, but I looked again at Puck as I responded.

"Because I don't trust him."

Crisp's eyes widened in surprise.

"Why not?"

"You know, Crisp, I'm not quite sure what your role is here."

This infuriated her. She stamped her foot.

"I'm here to protect Puck. Nobody else will."

I leaned across the desk and offered the envelope to Puck. Crisp reached for it, so I snatched it back. I glared at her, and she sat down.

"I'm also here to protect Miss Wren. That means *she* gets the check. She can do whatever she wants with it after she leaves my office."

The storm that had propelled Crisp into my office had blown out. She folded her arms across her chest and sulked. I held the check out again and Puck, after a moment's hesitation, leaned forward to accept it. She didn't open it or verify its contents before folding it in half and putting it in her white sequined purse.

I leaned back and looked at them like a pair of undecided jurors.

"Now, what are you two really doing here?"

They appeared surprised by my question, even though I thought they must have expected it, or even hoped I would ask it.

"Puck, are you…"

I paused and feigned an effort to find the right word.

"Are you comfortable living with Mr. Kuhl?"

Puck's brow furrowed.

"Of course. Why not? He's been good to me."

"You can leave, you know. You're over eighteen. No one can hold you against your will."

"Uncle Tommy's not holding me against my will. He's given me a place to stay until I get it together."

"Why do you call him Uncle Tommy?"

"Because he's my mother's brother."

It was my turn to be shocked. I had assumed that the tale of the family connection was a canard Kuhl had cooked up to cover a shameful relationship with this vulnerable young girl.

"You mean you're there voluntarily?"

"Of course. Didn't Mr. Crowley tell you that?"

I liked to tell myself that I only reached a conclusion when the facts I had gathered supported it, but I knew better. I had a nasty habit of letting personal judgment color my thinking. This was part of the reason that Heather would always be a better lawyer than me.

"I'm sorry. I misunderstood."

But it was worse than that: I had taken an instant dislike to Kuhl, and I'd let my animus drive my assessment of him.

Puck folded her hands. A gravely serious expression came over her small features.

"I know what you mean. He's not comfortable with me, either."

"Then, why are you living with him?"

She glanced again at Crisp, then took a breath.

"My parents aren't together. My mom got married…"

She stopped there and Crisp picked up the tale.

"To a monster!"

She stopped, searched for a word, then shook her head, too troubled to say any more.

"Is that true, Puck?"

Her eyes drooped and her voice became a whisper.

"Yes, it's true. That's why I ran away. Uncle Tommy found out where I was and gave me a safe place to live and a chance to get on my feet. That's what I'm doing."

"But you say you're not comfortable with each other."

"Tommy is only comfortable with things that have four legs and can be shot."

Crisp was trying to maintain a role in the discussion, but we both ignored her. Puck smiled as if she and I finally understood each other.

"I get the sense that you came here for more than the paycheck."

Puck studied her hands for a long moment, then looked at me.

"Mr. Proctor, do the police think Uncle Tommy had anything to do with what happened to Mr. Hamburger?"

"I don't know, Puck. They might. Why?"

"Because I know he didn't."

"How do you know that?"

"Because the person who carried the body through the woods and put it against the tree was a tall, thin man."

"You saw it?"

"No."

"Then, how do you know?"

"Uncle Tommy saw him. He told me."

I glanced at Crisp. I wanted to follow up, but this wasn't Puck's evidence. It was Tommy's. And who could predict what Puck might say in front of Crisp, the ultimate wild card?

I held up a hand to stop her.

"Have you told anybody about this?"

She shook her head.

"Not even the police?"

"They haven't asked me."

I gave Puck a probing look, then stood up.

"I think that's enough for today. Do you have a cell phone, Puck?"

She nodded, and I got her to air drop her contact information.

I walked them through the door and out to the parking lot, where I thanked them for coming with a mechanical formality that must have been off-putting, but it was the best I could manage under the circumstances.

Chapter Twenty-Seven

Another Shoe Drops

I found DP in his second floor aerie, busy on his PC, but he spun his chair as soon as he noticed my unannounced entrance. He assessed my expression and assumed his characteristic pose: feet crossed on his desk with his hands folded behind his head.

"I'm not sure if what you're about to tell me is good or bad."

"Me neither."

He took a bottle of water and tossed it to me, waiting while I unscrewed the cap and took a drink.

"Okay, let's hear it."

In as few words as possible, I delivered Puck's bombshell. DP watched me for a moment as he chose his words.

"Did you follow up with her?"

"No."

"Why not?"

I explained Crisp's presence and my caution about any disclosure made in her presence.

"That's sensible. So, what's bothering you?"

Friend in the Bullseye

I paused to let my thoughts coalesce.

"It's every lawyer's dream, I guess. I have too many clients. I owe them all a duty of honesty, but I know better than to tell them everything I learned working for one of the others."

"I get it. You need what they call 'plausible deniability.'"

"Isn't that a military term?"

"It can be. What it means is, what you don't know can't hurt you."

"Are you talking about my clients or me?"

He chuckled.

"Both, I guess."

"So, what's next?"

"You want me to go over there and have a talk with her? Find out exactly what Tommy told her?"

"I don't know. She's fragile and insecure. I don't want her to close down on us."

"Someone's got to find out what she knows."

"Let me give it a day or two."

"Joth, you don't have a day or two. You need to figure this out before the election."

I lapsed into silence, seeking a way to approach Puck without putting her off. DP let me sit before interrupting my thoughts.

"Well, I've got some news for you."

"Let's have it."

He gestured for me to sit beside him where I could view his PC. With a few clicks, he called up the Fairfax County Bar Directory and paged down to the M's. He stopped and backed his chair away. What I saw took my breath away. On the screen was a photograph of an attractive, dark-haired woman about my age.

"Beth McGillis?"

"Yup."

"She's a lawyer?"

"Yes. She does elder law for a small Fairfax firm."

DP shook his head as I struggled to fit the pieces together.

"She wasn't expelled from law school?"

"No. She graduated with her class."

"You sure this is the same person? The woman who used to go by Phyllis Doyle?"

"Definitely."

"What happened?"

"A lot of what Missy told you is true. She just mixed up the players. It wasn't Phyllis Doyle who got expelled. It was Missy."

"Missy was the cheat?"

"Seems like it."

"I thought she wasn't in that class?"

"They purged her off the roll."

"So, if Hamburger's girlfriend was expelled for cheating…"

"That part is true. Missy was dating Hamburger."

I sat down, thinking for a second it might be time for a stiff drink.

"You know, DP, I can deal with a guilty client. What I can't handle is a client who lies to me."

"You gonna fire her?"

"Not until I figure out what happened."

Further discussion was interrupted by Marie's voice on the intercom.

"Is Mr. Proctor up there?"

I spoke up to tell her I was.

"Ms. Brewer is here."

"Does she have an appointment?"

"I don't have one listed. Do you want me to put her in your office?"

"No, send her up here."

I wanted to do everything I could to snap Missy's icy confidence, and DP and his dim, forbidding office could help.

The woman who pushed open the door looked like she'd aged a year in less than 24 hours. She looked from DP to me. I stood up.

"Come in, Missy. This is DP Tran. He's my investigator."

She nodded, as if this was grim news and more was coming.

She sat down and fished inside her oversized purse, pulling out a rectangle of heavy paper, like the one Heather had received and I had seen on Jimmie Flambeau's desk. I took it from her and looked at it carefully: the same announcement of the 40th birthday surprise; the same requirement of punctual attendance, and the same promise of the Grand Reveal.

"You know anything about this?" she said.

She studied my expression.

"Nope."

She didn't respond until she'd finished searching my face. She was in the business of judging credibility. I hoped I'd passed.

"Well, I'm not going."

I looked again at the invitation, searching for any variation in form or content from the one Heather had shown me. As far as I could tell, they were identical.

"Somebody wants you to be there," said DP.

"That's why I'm not going."

She took the invitation back and looked at it as if it held hidden answers to unspoken questions.

"Did Hamburger dump you before or after he turned you in for cheating?"

She looked up. She seemed unsurprised by the question, as if she'd been waiting for me to figure it out. She spoke quietly while looking at her hands.

"It was after."

"I'm surprised you let him get the better of you."

"I should have just let it go."

"How'd you do it? Cheat, I mean?"

She gave DP a hard, appraising look before speaking.

"There was someone in the registrar's office."

"Who did you know there?"

"I didn't know anybody. But he did."

"He? Randy?"

"Yes."

"He told you that?"

"I don't remember him telling me that, but I guess he did."

"Then what happened?"

DP took another bottle of water from the minifridge, but Missy shook her head.

"Got anything stronger?"

"I think so. Bourbon?"

She nodded.

DP found a cocktail glass in his credenza, cleaned it with a swipe of a cloth napkin, and poured her a double shot. She took a long drink.

"Exams were coming up. I was a nervous wreck of course, and Randy noticed."

"Why were you nervous?"

"Because I was going to flunk the exam!"

"And?"

I sat back, folded my hands, and waited for her to gather her thoughts.

"The night before the exam, he came by my apartment. He had a sheet with five questions on it. He said that three of them would be on the exam, but the professor hadn't selected the final questions yet. So, we studied from the sheet."

"And the exam?"

"Totally different."

"Different? You mean different questions?"

"Yes."

"And?"

"And I panicked."

"And Randy?"

"He did fine. Me? I flunked. I probably would have flunked anyway."

"You flunked out of law school?"

"No. They found the questions in my backpack."

"Who?"

"The exam proctor. There would have been a trial, I guess, but when they saw my grade, they didn't bother. I told the school I'd withdraw, which is what I did. None of it ever touched Randy. I was stupid. I was naïve."

"But you did it."

"Yes."

"And Randy let you take the hit?"

"Let me take the hit? He set the whole thing up, Randy put the questions in my backpack, and then he told the proctor where to find them."

"That's a lot of trouble for him to get rid of a girlfriend."

"He wanted to date Phyllis. She wouldn't have anything to do with him, but he figured that with me out of the way . . . well, who knows."

So, there it was: a motive to kill. I was livid.

"Why didn't you tell me this from the start?"

"Because I know it looks bad."

"You think it looks better now?"

"When's the last time you spoke to her?"

Missy looked at DP.

"Phyllis? I don't know. We were friends, but the cheating thing put an end to that. You can understand."

"You didn't see her after that summer?"

"Some. Our lease expired in September. I went by to pick up my deposit. Larry had moved in with her at that point."

"Who's Larry?"

"Larry McGillis. She used to joke that she couldn't marry him because she'd be Phyllis McGillis."

"So, she changed her name?"

"Larry insisted. She hated Phyllis anyway. Beth's her middle name."

She took a long pull of the bourbon. I looked again at the invitation.

"You've been in touch with her. Probably still are."

She shook her head vehemently.

"I'm not. She didn't want to be associated with me."

She let her head wag, beaten down.

I suddenly felt a degree of sympathy for Missy. She may have lacked a functioning moral compass, but she had carved her own path in life through a formidable combination of grit and resilience. I found within myself a modicum of admiration for her, despite my contempt for her personal standards.

"Okay, Missy. All this is helpful. Let me think about it."

"What about the party?"

I glanced at DP. His face was impassive. It was clear that somebody wanted to confront Heather and Missy together and it was probably Sue Crandall. Forcing Missy to face her old roommate and her sordid past was just the sort of dramatic conclusion that could create a favorable impression with the public. Heather could fend for herself, but there were a dozen ways this could go south for Missy.

Before I could answer, DP spoke up.

"You should go."

This wasn't his call, and I looked at him sharply.

"Somebody's gone to a lot of trouble to set this up, Joth. We need to know who and why."

"I think we know who and I think we know why."

He shook his head.

"We don't know anything. You think Crandall's behind this? Well, it's better than responding to an arrest warrant. If it's Sue, don't forget, she'll be under the microscope, too. We can play this to our advantage."

"That's the dumbest idea you've ever had."

"Is it? We've got to break this logjam sooner or later, Joth. Why not Saturday night?"

I turned it over in my mind. There was logic in what he said. All ropes look like a lifeline when the ship is going down. It made sense to grab at this one.

Chapter Twenty-Eight

Cold Cider

Jenny Wren was an island of credibility in a sea of deceit. Even Heather wasn't above shading the facts when it served her purpose. In comparison to everyone else I'd dealt with in this case, Jenny seemed as pure as the season's first snow.

I believed she had told the truth about her Uncle Tommy, but I didn't know if he'd told the truth to his niece. If he'd seen someone propping Hamburger's body against the tree, why hadn't he reported this critical fact to the police?

Walking up Kuhl's leaf-strewn driveway as I thought it through, I heard a powerful engine roar. Kelleher pulled up beside me and rolled down the window of her cruiser. The late afternoon sun reflected off her Ray-Bans.

"He's not home."

"Who?"

She took her glasses off to make her skepticism obvious.

"I thought he was your client?"

"If he's my client, you shouldn't be talking to him without my permission."

The truth was, she didn't really believe I represented Tommy. The squad car had been idling and she turned it off.

"What about Missy Brewer?" she said. "One client per crime is the general rule."

"Is that why you referred Missy to me? Because you didn't want me representing someone else?"

"I don't care who you represent. But when you do, you need to make it plain."

"Then, let me make this plain, officer. Keep away from Tommy. Now, what did you want to ask him?"

"I think he's hiding something."

"What makes you think so?"

"Probably the same thing that brought you here today. Two years ago, he was sued by a neighbor in a boundary dispute. Turns out a good six feet of the land he thought was his actually belongs to that neighbor."

"So what?"

"It cost Tommy fifty grand in legal fees and sixty square feet of his property. So, who brought that suit? Randy Hamburger."

She tilted her head to assess my expression.

"You didn't know that did you?"

"What of it?"

"Well, you know it now. Let me know what excuse he makes if he gives you one."

She smiled as she re-started the car, indicating that she felt like she'd won this round, but there was something in it for me, too. I put my hand on the car door to keep her from moving.

"You and Crandall must be pretty friendly."

"It's a professional relationship, Joth."

"She got you out of the evidence room and back on the street."

"Where I'm a lot more valuable to the community."

"I was under the impression that she got you out of there because she wanted your help on the Hamburger case."

"So?"

"You were working street patrol the night of Tommy's party. She pulled you out before he was killed."

"Sue's the Chief Deputy. Chief Deputies always have a go-to cop they work with."

"Not in this county."

"Things are changing, Joth."

"You're going to need a better explanation than that."

She shrugged. I jerked my hand off the door as she rolled up the window and drove away.

I took everything Christine told me with a large grain of salt, but I was hoping she'd been truthful about

Tommy. It would be much easier to talk to Jenny if he wasn't around. I let the heavy knocker fall against the oak door. Jenny looked down from the casements above. I waited for her to let me in.

"Are you here to see Uncle Tommy?"

"No. I'm here to see you."

My answer elicited a shy smile. She wasn't used to personal visitors, and she was glad to have one. She ushered me into the library and offered me one of the red leather chairs.

"Cider?"

"Sure."

"Cold?"

"That would be great."

She left and returned quickly with a pair of copper mugs. She gave me one and took the chair on the other side of the fireplace. She was dressed in her customary white, but with none of the theatrical trappings I was used to. In white jeans and a turtleneck, she looked like any other 20-something I might pass on the street.

"No Crisp?"

She shook her head.

"Uncle Tommy doesn't like her."

"Why not?"

"I'm not sure. He doesn't trust her."

Those were two different answers, but I didn't think she was lying. She really wasn't sure. She sipped her cider.

"You haven't asked him?"

"Uncle Tommy's a hard man to talk to."

"What about you?

She shrugged. She was using her mug as a tiny shield, a buffer between us, or perhaps between me and what she was hesitating to say.

"Crisp is a little rough around the edges, isn't she?"

"Yes!"

She sounded relieved, as if she had stumbled onto a simple answer to a complex question that had been troubling her.

"How come you hang around with her?"

"She's been good to me. My only friend, really."

"A little bit smothering?"

"Yes, that's it."

She looked relieved.

I looked at my watch.

"Do you know when Tommy's coming back?"

"No. He said he had errands to run. That can mean anything."

"I wanted to ask him about something important. You said Tommy saw the person who propped the body against the tree. He told you that?"

She nodded and sipped.

"But you didn't see it? The person, I mean?"

"No."

"You said it was a tall, thin man. How did he know it was a man?"

She thought before she answered.

"He didn't exactly say it was a man. He said it was a tall, thin person that he thought was a man."

"How come you didn't offer this to the police?"

"Tommy was afraid for me."

"Afraid of what?"

She shrugged.

"I'm a little different, you know? Uncle Tommy was afraid the police might get the wrong idea about me."

"Well, I don't have the wrong idea."

"I know."

"Is there anything else you can tell me? Anything that might help?"

She thought about it and shook her head. There was more, but she wasn't ready to divulge it and I didn't want to push her. I didn't want to alienate the only pure truth teller in the case. I thanked her for her time, and the cider, and headed home.

Chapter Twenty-Nine

Light in the Fog

Saturday marked two weeks since Tommy Kuhl's party and Randy Hamburger's murder. The gray drizzle of the morning cleared by afternoon and warming air brought a low, swirling fog at sunset. It was already dark when Heather and I turned on to Balfour Circle. There were no streetlights in the cul de sac and the house at the back of the circle was dark.

1001: Beth McGillis's house.

I looked at my watch. We were ten minutes early.

"Is this the place?"

"I think so," said Heather. "It's been a while."

"You don't need to whisper."

I expected her to laugh at my comment, but she was in no mood for levity.

"Something's not right, Joth."

As I swung through the circle, my headlights focused on a three-story colonial without architectural distinction. A single light shown from the back of the first floor. It was the sort of light someone puts on a timer before leaving for vacation.

We parked, got out and walked back. The cul de sac was as quiet as the grave. I checked the mailbox for 1001: empty. There was no garage, no cars parked in front, and none of the spooky seasonal displays that engaged the creativity of most northern Virginia homeowners.

As I considered the possibilities, I heard Heather's voice from the driveway.

"Hey, look at this."

The trees behind the house were losing their leaves, but a thin canopy of decaying foliage remained. Heather noticed a glow from somewhere within them.

"Should we call the fire department?"

I thought about it.

"No. That's where the party is."

I used my flashlight to find the path I had discovered on the night of Tommy's party. A heavy ground fog swirled, reminiscent of the dry ice machines that pumped out a manufactured mist on that night, but this was the real thing.

Stepping slowly and quietly, I led Heather as we followed the damp, smokey scent of the fire. The glow increased around each bend. Past the last turn, we stepped into an empty, fog-shrouded clearing. The fire came from an untended firepit built into the center of an elaborate labyrinth. Its flat stones separated the leaf strewn, winding paths of the maze. Around the rim of the circle, eight tree stumps provided rustic seating. There was no wind, and the heavy, fragrant smoke from the fire drifted straight up.

"Kids?" said Heather.

An owl tracking us screeched from the trees.

"I don't know. I don't think so."

Heather sounded as uneasy as I felt. I took her hand and led her across the labyrinth. We sat on two of the stumps, facing the spot where the path entered the circle. The flickering fire cut the chill and the atmosphere would have been cozy if not for a sense that we were seated at the center of a web of death and deceit.

"What do we do now?"

"We wait."

We didn't have to wait long. The next sound we heard was unmistakable. Someone else was following the glow from the cul de sac, just as we had. Whoever it was stopped just outside the circle of light. Heather and I exchanged glances. Then Missy Brewer appeared through the fog.

"Hello Joth."

"I though you weren't coming."

Her eyes scanned the circle and the surrounding woods.

"I couldn't resist."

Friend in the Bullseye

Of course not. Only a person with no stake in the case could afford to ignore the invitation.

Heather was seated two stumps to my right. As Missy sat down on a stump to my left, I introduced them with minimal explanation, and they exchanged frosty acknowledgements.

"What are we waiting for?" said Missy.

"We're waiting for the host to show up."

As if on cue, Heather raised her chin and a finger. Someone was approaching. Following the sound of crumpling leaves and twigs, I realized this individual was entering from the other end of the path through the woods, so when Tommy Kuhl emerged, I was not surprised.

He was dressed in fatigue pants, a camo military jacket and a black ball cap pulled low over his eyes. Slung over his shoulder was a composite hunting bow and a quiver of arrows. He stood at the edge of the circle and watched us, like a hunter stalking game.

"Good evening, Tommy. What are you doing here?"

Stepping into the firelight, he held up a heavily creased copy of the same invitation Heather and Missy had received.

"Is this from you?"

"No," I said. "But it's what brought us all here."

He cautiously sat on a stump across the circle from me.

"What's it mean?"

"That's what we're here to find out."

Tension limited our sporadic conversation. Heather and Tommy exchanged banal pleasantries in terse whispers. I listening to the woods. We seemed to have disturbed the local denizens. Small woodland animals scurried in the undergrowth. When I heard the movement of something larger, I held up a hand and the conversation paused. Sharp breaths were inhaled.

Frank Moran emerged into the circle. He was jittery and stumbled on the uneven stones along the labyrinth pathway. I got up and grabbed his arm. He was dressed for a nor'easter in an orange anorak over a wool turtleneck and he was babbling nonsense under his breath.

Alarmed, I looked for injuries before remembering Heather's comment on rumors of substance abuse. His breath reeked of alcohol. Frank was as drunk as a sailor on Saturday night. I planted him on the stump immediately to my right.

"Sit right down here, Frank."

He lowered himself gingerly. Once he got settled, I held Heather's invitation in front of his face and made him focus on it.

"Did you get one of these, Frank?"

It took him a moment to comprehend the question. When he did, he nodded.

I stretched my back and sat down, wondering who would be next.

It was someone I expected because I'd seen the invitation on his desk: Jimmie Flambeau, dapper in a black sweater and pants. His eyes traveled the circle and settled on me. He smiled like he was in on the joke.

"I thought I might find you here."

"I'm surprised you showed up."

"Never turn your back on free information, Joth."

"Information? Are we expected to gather it or disclose it?"

Before anyone could respond, I heard another familiar voice. So did Heather.

Sue Crandall took a moment to assess the scene before she strode confidently toward the firepit. She looked like a child on Christmas morning who finds all her wishes fulfilled under the tree.

"Hello, Sue. Is this your party?"

"Me? Sorry, Joth, you've confused me with someone else."

"Did you send these invitations?"

"No. But I got one."

She held it up as if it was her passport into this motley assembly. As she did, she looked around the circle again.

"Somebody has gone to a lot of trouble. Everyone my office has associated with Hamburger's murder is here."

"Does that include you, Sue?"

She ignored Heather's barb, as I expected.

"You think all this drama is going to help you get my office?"

"Shut up, Heather."

I'm sure that no subordinate, in fact very few people at all, had ever spoken to Heather that way. I stepped in before she could react.

"How'd you find your way back here, Sue?"

She shrugged.

"The house looked empty," she said. "I saw a light, so I followed it."

It was a sensible mantra for a prosecutor. It occurred to me that everything would be simpler if she lived by it. She sat down with the air of a monarch.

"Joth, if you didn't organize this, who did?"

"I did."

The voice belonged to DP Tran. He stepped into the circle of light cast by the firepit.

He was dressed like a burglar, with black ninja pants and a black, military grade shirt. He moved with the confident swagger of a man accustomed to dubious scenes and unsettled scores.

"I'm sorry for the inconvenience, everyone. You especially, Joth, but sometimes what you don't know can't hurt you. Or your clients. When I found out McGillis and her family had gone on a holiday cruise, I saw an opportunity. I'm the one who sent the invitations."

"How'd you know it's her birthday?"

"It's not. It's her husband's. So what? They're gone."

"What kind of a crazy…"

"You said it yourself, Ms. Crandall. All the suspects are here. Don't bother to thank me. It's time to answer the questions we've all been asking. This is the night to do it, and this is exactly the right place."

DP sat down, and Tommy stood up. The great white hunter had displayed a fidgety discomfort since entering the circle.

"I don't know anything about this," he said. "I'm leaving."

"Go ahead."

But he hesitated and the moment was lost. Tommy was as curious as the rest of us, and like a moth, he was compelled to the flame. He sat back down.

"I've got nothing to do with this."

"Really?" said Sue.

"I was throwing a party."

Sue assumed an indignant expression. Tommy was a guy who talked too much when he was anxious. Sue was baiting him.

"Yes, you were intimately involved in setting up the party, weren't you? People checked with you before placing their ghouls and cadavers around your yard. You reserved a special tree for Hamburger, and you knew just when the time was right to haul the body out of the woods and place him there. I figure you needed fifteen minutes max for that and to get back to the party."

"I had no reason to kill Randy Hamburger."

"A lie," said Sue. "He brought a suit against you two years ago and it hit you where it hurts. You lost a strip of your property to a neighbor. And plenty of money, too."

Tommy Kuhl, the man with a reputation for killing big game with a composite bow, looked unnerved.

"If everyone Randy Hamburger sued had a motive to kill him, you'll have to consider a long list," I said.

"But why would you lie about it?" Sue said. "And then there's the toy arrow stuck to Hamburger's chest. The signature of the great bow hunter, no?"

"No."

"That's enough, Sue," I said. "Tommy's not here to be cross-examined."

At least I didn't want Sue grilling him. I turned to Tommy, recalling what Puck had told me the previous afternoon.

"You didn't kill him, Tommy. But you did see the person who placed his body against the tree."

He wrestled with the question before providing a tentative answer.

"That may be true."

Tommy was startled by the extent of my knowledge. Recognizing this, the two prosecutors sat up. Tommy's eyes blinked in the firelight, wary about what else I knew.

"You thought it was a man."

He nodded.

"I said I thought it was a man, but I'm not sure. I wasn't sure then. There was something odd about the way he moved. I didn't think anything of it at the time. Everyone was having a good time. Such a very good time."

"Why did you lie to the police?"

Sue's voice rose in anger, but understanding Tommy's motive, I answered for him.

"You were afraid it might have been your niece."

"No. Jenny was dressed in white. It was someone dressed all in black."

He eyed DP threateningly.

"Dressed like a ninja."

This challenge sapped the last bit of Tommy's energy. He let his head hang, not to mourn the murder victim, but the ruin of his carefully planned social event.

Sue glanced at DP before her eyes locked in on the other person dressed all in black. She got to her feet, leveling a finger at Jimmie as if singling out the culprit for the jury.

"Randy Hamburger campaigned on a platform of aggressive law enforcement that would have put your world at risk. You couldn't let him win."

I knew something that Sue could only guess at. Jimmie had pegged Hamburger as the likely winner and had developed his odds accordingly, but he wasn't dumb enough to admit any of that to Sue Crandall. And Sue didn't necessarily care. As far as she was concerned, Hamburger's strict law and order stance provided sufficient motive.

Jimmie just smiled.

"I keep my hands out of politics," he said. "Except that I give generously to all the candidates."

Sue's face tightened. She was like a hungry person at an all-you-can eat buffet. Each alternative was more tempting than the last. She spun around to confront Missy.

"And what about you? Hamburger turned you in for cheating on an exam, bringing your legal career to a crashing end before it even started. Let bygones be bygones? I don't think so. You threatened his life on your radio show."

I had Sue pegged as a dilettante, someone seduced by the lure of the CA's office, but uninterested in the hard work it demanded. Her attention jumped to address each new theory or revelation as it emerged, but she was bristling like a rottweiler.

I began to wonder if I'd been wrong about her.

"I had no access to poison," said Missy. "And I wouldn't know what to do with it if I did."

I'd been so focused on Missy's deceitfulness that I'd missed this obvious point. She had a motive to kill Randy Hamburger, but she lacked the means.

"She's just a noisy windbag," said Tommy.

It was a powerful retort because it was simple and true. Missy was loud and abrasive, but her vehemence was just a shield for her insecurity. Tonight, she looked small and fragile. Sue quickly processed this, regrouped and started again.

"But Heather Burke did," said Sue. "Heather, you had unrestricted access to the evidence room, and you were sure to lose your job after the votes were counted on Tuesday. You had the means, and you had the motive. You'd take that to a grand jury, wouldn't you Heather?"

Heather merely rolled her eyes.

"Be careful, Sue," I said. "Before you know it, you'll make a case against yourself. You always wanted Heather's job. How far are you willing to go to get it?"

"I don't want her job."

"Of course, you do" Heather said. "And your ambition is blinding you to the facts that are right in front of you. You had access to the evidence room."

"Stop worrying, Heather. I'm after the Fairfax job, the biggest jurisdiction in the state."

"You don't live in Fairfax County."

"I've got my eye on a house out there. I'm hoping I'll get your support."

I thought that was likely. There were few things Heather wanted more than to be rid of Sue Crandall.

"And after this case, that job will be mine."

I looked around for DP, but he had vanished.

Chapter Thirty

The Grand Reveal

Sue Crandall had taken control.

"I'm ready to air all facts and arguments. The killer is here, and we will name him, or her…"

She aimed a sharp look at Heather.

"…before we leave here tonight."

I searched the faces around the circle again. The pieces were beginning to fall together.

"You're right, Sue, but you're also wrong. DP gathered five people, all of whom had either the motive, means, or opportunity to kill Randy Hamburger, but none of them had all three. So, where does that put us?"

As the invitees pondered this question, my eyes settled on Frank Moran. Sensing the scrutiny, he ran his hands through his disheveled hair as he broke eye contact with me.

"How about a man who made his name investigating drug crimes? A man who knew his way around the evidence room."

"This is absurd. What did Frank have against Randy Hamburger?" said Sue.

I looked at him.

"Why don't you tell them, Frank?"

He squirmed on the stump and said nothing.

"Frank had the motive, Sue," I said. "It was Randy Hamburger who caught him tampering with evidence."

Heather, staring hard at Moran as if seeing him for the first time, picked up the story.

"That's right. Woodbury. It was a cocaine case. Possession with intent to distribute."

I nodded.

"Frank thought it would end up in a plea, but the defense was ready to take it to a jury. It turned out that the coke entered into evidence was a good bit less than the amount that had been impounded from Woodbury. The Commonwealth had to drop the case, which led to an internal affairs investigation. You got demoted."

Heather nodded as she remembered. She picked up the story.

"The defense attorney was Randy Hamburger. What about it, Frank? You were on the way out and you knew it. "

"I have an alibi."

I remembered our lunch at Il Radiccio. He told me he had been in Ireland at the time of Hamburger's murder. Now, he said it again.

"I was in the Auld Sod. I have receipts."

Friend in the Bullseye

The momentum and energy dissipated with Frank's response. Sue seemed doubtful and a collective uncertainty bred a self-defensive hostility within the group. Accusatory and wary glances were exchanged. Fingers were pointed, eyebrows raised.

Heather stood up, ready to speak, but was stopped by a commotion in the bushes. DP pushed into the circle, propelling someone before him with her arm bent up behind her back. He shoved her to the ground in front of the firepit.

It was Crisp.

"Here's the person we want to talk to. Tommy, is this the person who put Hamburger's body against the tree?"

Tommy looked at her, then dropped his eyes.

"It might have been her. I thought it was just another dummy."

Sue was skeptical.

"You think this sack of shit killed Randy Hamburger?"

"She did," I said. "But she needed help. She was glad to get it from somebody who hated him almost as much as she did."

Crisp stood up, snarling like an angry coyote, looking for a way out of a trap.

"I have an alibi," said Frank.

But his voice had lost its confident timbre.

"Sure," I said.

I thought back to our lunch, when Frank had denied seeing me at Riding Time.

"Frank. Have you got those airplane receipts? When did you leave for Ireland?"

Some of the confidence returned to his voice. This was a fortress he could fight from.

"October 18. And I didn't come back until after the death."

I had brought Heather's print-out of evidence room activity. I pulled it out of my jacket pocket and tilted it toward the firelight to scan it.

"Frank Moran, the smiling Irishman who hates to fly but makes his first trip to the Emerald Isle during the week Hamburger is murdered. You might have been in Ireland when Hamburger died, but you signed into the evidence room the day before you left."

"So what?"

"For you, it was personal, Frank. But that wasn't what motivated Crisp. Hamburger opposed everything you stand for, Crisp. There'd be no place in Arlington County for someone like you if he was enforcing the law."

She pointed a long, boney finger at Frank.

"I don't know him. How would I know a cop?"

"Because Frank had been shifted to vice as his punishment for the Woodbury debacle. I've represented Riding Time for years. Every new vice cop gets to know Dan and his girls. It's an easy beat. You keep your eyes open for drug deals and prostitution, and you enjoy a cold beer at the end of the day, courtesy of Irish Dan Crowley. A gregarious guy like Frank is always ready to chat up the girls. Especially if he finds one of Irish heritage, like the former Chester Kelly."

"That's not true."

"But it is. And the rest of it is simple. Crisp, you learned about the party from Puck, and you knew who would be there. You told Frank, and then Frank had an idea. He explained to you how to deliver the strychnine before he got on the plane. You took it from there."

"I wasn't at the party."

The weird falsetto was gone from her voice. She sounded just like any other angry man.

"Yes, you were."

Puck had stepped onto the edge of the circle so quietly that no one had noticed.

"You were there," she said. "You were the mummy."

"Tommy," I said, "the person you saw dressed all in black propping the body against the tree wasn't a ninja. It was a tall, thin woman wrapped in black bandages. A mummy."

He processed this, then nodded slowly.

"The final brick in the wall!" said Sue.

As she got up and stepped aggressively forward, Crisp shied away. Then, with a quick movement of her right hand, she threw something into the fire pit and a shattering explosion followed a flash of light. She fled in the confusion, with Tommy and me on her tail.

Crisp was quicker than she looked. She abandoned the path and broke into the woods like a deer. I left her to Tommy. When I got back to the circle, I told Sue to call 911.

"I already did. She won't get far. Now, I want some answers."

"The answer's right in front of you, Sue."

Frank had taken advantage of the chaos to attempt his own escape. He didn't get far. DP forced him back into the circle, where he sank down on his stump, a defeated man at last.

"Frank, you've been skimming cocaine for years," I said. "You had regular access to the evidence room, and sometimes...well, a little bit of coke wouldn't be missed, especially if the case didn't go to trial. You knew how to get small amounts of contraband out without leaving a trace. And you knew how to get large amounts out as well. You figured no one was going to open the Luigi file again."

"That's nonsense."

"I don't think so, Frank. You fell into the trap of ready access. It cost you your job and your reputation, and you're not the sort of guy to let that lie. You had to have your revenge on the man who turned on you. And that man was Randy Hamburger."

I glanced at Heather, who was paying close attention to my every word. I almost smiled at her as I pivoted to face Sue Crandall.

"You following this, Sue? With that Irish temper of yours, you weren't going to let it go. Especially when you knew someone who hated him even more than you did."

I was just warming up when Tommy re-entered, pushing Crisp ahead of him. She hissed at him like a snake.

"I've never shot any living thing in my life. Even those heads hanging in my library were shot by my guide. But I'm willing to shoot you."

He had fitted one of those deadly bolts into the slide of his crossbow and looked like he meant to use it.

Crisp watched him and seethed like a wildcat, but the fight was over.

"For Frank, it was revenge. Crisp liked hanging around Kuhl's place because she liked the cushy lifestyle or because she liked Puck. Probably both. You got her the strychnine, Frank. You explained how and when to administer it and headed off to Ireland. Did you put it in his cough medicine?"

Frank tilted his head to peer at me but ignored the question.

Sue hadn't called 911. Instead, she'd called her personal deputy, Christine Kelleher. She arrived in full uniform with a service revolver on her hip. She pointed at Moran and then Crisp.

"Officer, take their phones and see if anyone's armed."

Moran gave up his phone without protest and Kelleher found a revolver inside his jacket. She took it out, inspected it and pocketed it.

"You're going to need back-up, Christine. There's two of them."

"Back up's on the way."

Neither of them was about to go anywhere but jail. Frank, a tired, drunken man, was whipped. Crisp took a long look at Tommy's crossbow and submitted without further resistance. Before Christine could cuff them both, we heard sirens from the cul de sac. The back-up followed the path back to the labyrinth and took the two killers away.

Chapter Thirty-One

Coffee and Tea

It couldn't have worked out better for Sue Crandall. It was her case, and Heather let her roll with it. For 48 hours, the double arrest got top coverage in the local media, and Sue handled it with aplomb, building the resume she hoped would propel her to the Fairfax job.

We had her press conference on TV in DP's office.

"I hope the Fairfax County voters are watching," said Heather.

"It's a long time until the next election."

She sipped her coffee.

"Yeah, but now Sue and I understand each other. I am looking forward to the next election, though."

DP had been in court for the bond hearings that morning. Frank Moran surrendered his passport and considering his long residence and service to the community, his bond was set at $100,000. The judge fixed bond at $75,000 for Christine Kelly and they were both languishing in jail. Jimmie Flambeau returned quietly to his seedy underworld and Tommy Kuhl was said to be on a safari in Africa. And then there was Missy.

When Sue's presser ended, DP looked at his watch.

"You know what time it is, children? It's Missy Brewer time!"

He flipped on the radio and tuned in to her show. Missy's guest was an adjunct criminal law professor at a school I'd never heard of.

"They're all incompetents," Missy said.

"That's the problem! Idealistic first-year law students soon hear the siren song of big business and big money. The talent goes there, and our criminal justice system caters to the rich and powerful."

Missy agreed.

"As I know from first-hand experience! It was obvious from the beginning who the killers were."

"And you told this to the police?"

"Of course. You know how it is. They'll do whatever they can to protect one of their own. I was dragged through the coals because they wanted to shut me up. But that will never…"

Rolling her eyes, Heather reached over and turned off the radio. I walked to the credenza and poured myself another cup of coffee.

Missy Brewer was full of surprises, but this was not one of them. I knew I'd cross paths with Jimmie, Irish Dan, and even Tommy Kuhl again, but I hoped I'd seen the last of the Brewer of Mischief.

About the Author

James V. Irving was born and raised in Gloucester, Massachusetts. He is a graduate of the University of Virginia (UVA), where he majored in English. He holds a law degree from the College of William and Mary and is a member of the bars of Virginia, Maryland, the District of Columbia and Massachusetts.

After completing his undergraduate studies at UVA, Mr. Irving spent two years employed as a private detective in Northern Virginia, where he pursued wayward spouses, located skips, investigated insurance claims and handled criminal investigations. In his early years as a lawyer, he practiced criminal law, which along with his investigative experience and trial work, informs this fictional account of Joth Proctor.

Upcoming New Release!

JAMES V. IRVING'S

NO FRIEND OF THINE
A JOTH PROCTOR FIXER MYSTERY
BOOK 6

Antiquities dealer Micah Hornblower acquires a rare copy of a sixteenth century play that may have been signed by the author—William Shakespeare. The evidence indicates that the signature is a phony, but a frightening demand for the book sends Hornblower to Joth Proctor for advice…. Unsure of exactly what they have or why it's worth a man's life, Joth and DP Tran retain the book in the face of both legal and extralegal efforts to obtain it.…

When Joth and DP learn the true source of the book's value, they realize both lives and the judgment of history are at stake.

**For more information
visit:** www.SpeakingVolumes.us

Now Available!

JAMES V. IRVING
JOTH PROCTOR FIXER MYSTERIES
Books 1 - 4

"Irving's writing is relaxed and authentic and takes readers inside a compelling world of legal and social issues..." —Bruce Kluger, columnist, USA Today

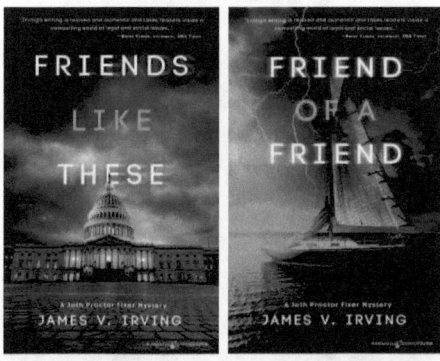

**For more information
visit: www.SpeakingVolumes.us**

Now Available!

MATTHEW J. FLYNN

BERNIE WEBER: MATH GENIUS SERIES
Books 1 - 3

**For more information
visit:** www.SpeakingVolumes.us

Now Available!

BRIEN A. ROCHE

THE PROHIBITION SERIES
Books 1 – 3

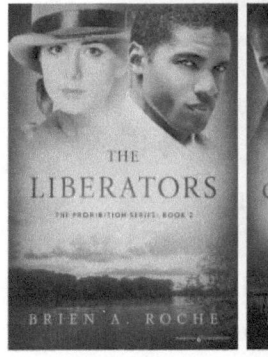
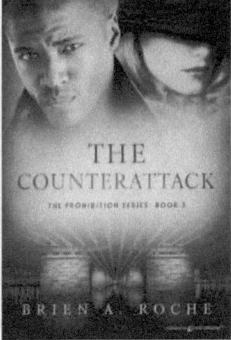

**For more information
visit:** www.SpeakingVolumes.us

Now Available!

JACQUE ROSMAN

MURDER IN GEORGETOWN
The Academic Mom Mysteries
Books 1

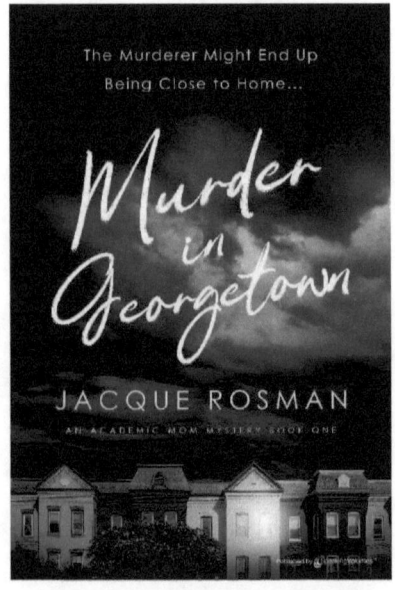

**For more information
visit:** www.SpeakingVolumes.us

www.ingramcontent.com/pod-product-compliance
Lightning Source LLC
LaVergne TN
LVHW041700060526
838201LV00043B/500